CUSHLA

Memoirs of a Reluctant Gypsy Girl

ELIZABETH RADMORE

Published by

 GENERAL STORE
GSPH PUBLISHING HOUSE

499 O'Brien Road, Box 415
Renfrew, Ontario, Canada K7V 4A6
Telephone (613) 432-7697 or 1-800-465-6072

ISBN 1-897113-04-8
Printed and bound in Canada

Cover Painting by: Elizabeth Radmore
Original design by: George McKnight
Cover design and layout by: Custom Printers
Author Photo: Dave Norton

General Store Publishing House
Renfrew, Ontario, Canada

Library and Archives Canada Cataloguing in Publication

Radmore, Elizabeth
        Cushla: memoirs of a reluctant Gypsy girl / Elizabeth Radmore

ISBN 1-897113-04-8

        1. Romanies—Ireland—Fiction. I. Title.

PS8635.A36C8 2004   C813'.6   C2004-906465-7

I wish to dedicate this book to my mother,

who was the story's inspiration,

and to my father,

who was a great storyteller, himself.

To Matilox
Enjoy!
Elizabeth Roomore

ONE

It was Friday, the first of September, 1953, and like every other Friday night, my mother prepared an Ulster fry for supper. The sun was shining and the weather was unusually mild for that time of the year.

In the days before my father lost his job, my brothers and I looked forward to him exuberantly bursting through the door on Friday, picking one of us up and swinging the lucky one in the air. Then we'd line up for our weekly thruppence. With a playful look on his face my father would ask, "Is it yer pay yer after?" Giggling at the sheer predictability of the ritual we'd reply, "Yes, Da, it is."

As soon as the thruppences were placed in our hands and a hasty "Thanks, Da!" had been uttered, we'd light out for the corner shop. Upon our return home, we'd put our sweets on top of the piano for after supper. Those days were filled with happiness and laughter.

But things changed when my father lost his job. Then, Fridays were a sad reminder that there was no payday. There was a lot less laughter, no lighthearted conversation at the supper table and no sweets to tempt us from the piano.

After a couple of months, there came a Friday when my father was even more subdued. He ate his fried soda bread, sausages, and "dippy" eggs in silence. He was tense and distracted. He slurped his strong sweet tea noisily and set the mug on the table in front of him. Clasping his hands in front of him he looked directly at my mother and in a soft but determined voice said that he had made a decision. He was going to leave on Monday morning to look for work. There was nothing in Belfast.

I shared a bed with my brother David, and that night I feigned sleep so that he wouldn't talk to me. When I was sure he was asleep, I got out of bed and knelt down beside it. With my hands clasped under my chin and my eyes shut tight, I pleaded with God to find my father a job so that he wouldn't have to leave us. In return I promised that I would be good and that I wouldn't tell any more lies or keep the penny that my mother gave me every Sunday for the collection box.

I climbed back into bed beside David. He was warm and sleeping soundly. He provided a great deal of comfort in the quiet darkness of that small room as I listened to my mother and father downstairs. They were talking about my father's decision, of course, and my mother kept blowing her nose and sniffling, so I knew she was crying.

I consoled myself with thoughts of life before this terrible calamity. My father was always joking and laughing with us and loving and helpful to my mother. But lately there were times when he didn't look so happy, sitting by the window alone with his thoughts.

I finally fell asleep, and it seemed only minutes before I heard the rattle of the milkman's cart.

I loved Saturdays. We were allowed to stay in bed as long as we liked. There was always a full pot of porridge on the stove, and since I was the last one out of bed, I just helped myself. After helping my mother with the housecleaning chores, I was free to play with my friends the rest of the day. This particular Saturday, however, turned out to be one of the worst days of my life.

I had just started playing my favourite game called "piggy and stick" with my friends on the cobblestone street in front of my house. Piggy and stick is a game that you play with a piece of wood, whittled to a point at both ends. It is put on the curb of the sidewalk with one end jutting out, and you give it a whack with another stick. The object of the game is to get the "piggy" as far across the street as possible. The winner is the first one to reach the other side.

We played in the middle of the street, because no one on Nore Street owned a car, and no one who owned one seemed to have friends to visit on Nore Street. However, on Saturdays street traffic could be busy with vendors selling their wares from carts, drawn by horses. The most dangerous hazard was the chance that we might step on one of the steaming, smelly ginger balls left by the horses.

My father, always ready with a joke or a funny story, some of which I heard many times, asked, "Did ya hear about wee ginger?" The first time he asked me this question, I answered, "No, Daddy, I didn't." "Well," he said, "he was lyin' smokin' in the middle of the road and got run over." As he walked away laughing, it dawned on me that he wasn't talking about a person at all, but the steaming horse dung flattened on the road.

On Saturdays there was an endless procession of horses and carts. The first to appear was the milkman, followed by the breadman and the fishmonger, whom you could smell before actually seeing. Albert, the ragman, was heard several streets away bellowing "any oul rags." The first couple of words were mumbled, but he would shout "rags" so loudly he could be heard inside your house with the door closed and the wireless blaring. The Saturday procession was usually brought to an end by the unmistakable rumbling and jangling of the ironmonger's cart as its wooden wheels clanged over the bumpy cobblestones.

Glancing over my shoulder as I took my turn at whacking the "piggy," I saw my father walking over towards me, his head bent and his hands shoved deep into his pockets.

He watched us for awhile, and then he said to me, "Come in the house for a wee minute, luv, I hafta talk t'ya."

"Ach, not right now, Daddy. It's my turn. I'll be in in a wee while."

"No, luv, yer ma and me need to talk to y'now." His voice was so gentle that I dropped the stick at once and followed him into the house with a sense of dread. Inside, he sat me down on the sofa in front of the soot-blackened fireplace just as gently and hunkered down in front of me. He took my two hands in his and looked directly into my eyes. I was the eldest, he said, and I was to go with him and look for a job as well. I didn't hear anything else he was saying. I knew he was still speaking because I could see his lips moving. I could feel heat from the fireplace, but I felt cold inside. My arms and legs felt suddenly heavy and numb. I was devastated at the thought of leaving my mother and finding a job. I felt as though a wave had crashed over me and swept me away.

I burst into tears and ran to my mother, who was in the scullery, standing hunched over the sink, staring down the drain hole. She was crying, too, and that was some comfort. Her eyes were red and swollen and her cheeks glistening with tears. She turned to me, and seeing the look of sadness and disbelief on my face, fell to her knees and folded her arms around me.

"I love you, Kathleen, I don't want t'let y'go, but I have no choice. Your da has t'find a job. There's nothin' around here. We need money comin' in t'survive and you're old enough nye t'be helpin' yer family.

"Your da's a smart man, and I'm sure it won't take long for him t'find work, and there's plenty o' flax mills would take on a young girl like you and train y'in the spinnin' and the weavin'. So don't worry, luv, when y'find jobs, yer brothers and me will come and join ye and we'll all be together again."

The thought of leaving my mother and my home and going to work tore into my heart. I followed her everywhere. No amount of begging and pleading on my part seemed able to change her mind about my going with my father. She said I should look on the bright side, that it would be an adventure; and then, tired of my persistence, she finally said, "Nye, Kathleen, at fourteen I was workin' in a factory, earnin' a wage and helpin' yer granny keep the house. Aye, I did, and that's not much older than you are now."

I tried to convince her that I should stay home and go to school. However, my mother was a very determined woman, and once a decision was made, nothing would change her mind.

I didn't feel I was ready to go to work. I wasn't ready to grow up yet. I had dreams of becoming an artist or an opera singer. I could be heard singing throughout the house, in a lilting high soprano trill and my mother would say.

"Hey, girl, who d'ya think y'are, Deanna Durbin?"

I knew in my heart that I did not want to slog it out long hours every day, six days a week in a mill or factory. Staying in school would have meant a better job.

A disturbing feeling hung over the weekend, like a black cloud ready to spill something dark and scary. I couldn't imagine what life would be like without my mother and my two brothers. My whole world revolved around my family and the house that I had lived my whole life in.

Two

The night before we left, I didn't sleep at all. When dawn's first light seeped through the window blind, I felt sick and choked with tears. I quietly slipped out of bed and tiptoed to the window and peered through the crack in the blind. It was a cold and misty September morning, even more damp and depressing than was usual for a September morning in Belfast.

No one was up yet, so I crept back into bed beside David. This time he didn't provide much comfort. I shivered and felt helpless and alone.

Too soon, I heard my mother calling us for breakfast.

We shared our last meal together in silence.

The only sound was the clink of the bowls of porridge being placed on the table before us. My mother was usually talkative and cheerful, but today she was pensive. There were deep furrows in her brow, and she struggled to swallow each spoonful of porridge. After breakfast, she helped me into my Burberry raincoat. Tears streamed down her face, and her hands trembled as she fastened up the buttons and tenderly placed and tied the belt around my waist.

When she finally spoke, her voice was husky from crying. Her eyes were red and swollen and glistening with tears. She murmured softly, "Be a good girl for your da, and remember I love you."

While my mother and father shared a tearful last kiss and embrace, I went to each of my brothers and kissed their cheeks and said goodbye. They didn't understand why I had to leave. They stood close together holding each other's hand, breaking their silence only to whisper goodbye.

Dropping his arms from around my mother, my father looked down at me, saying, "We'd better git goin', luv." I trembled as I stepped out the front door.

My Aunt Lily and a few neighbour women had bunched up and paid for a new pair of "white mutton dummies." They all agreed that I'd need good footwear for trampin' the land. With great sadness my mother had had to pawn the gold watch that belonged to her father. My father kept the ten pounds she had received—a grand sum of money—in his money belt, along with identification papers for both of us.

I could hardly believe this was really happening. As my father closed the door behind us, an empty, ominous feeling in the pit of my stomach made me feel like I could lose my breakfast at any moment. I would have, but for the small, sad crowd of well-wishers standing in front of the house—my Aunt Lily, Mrs. Hagan, Mrs. Donnelly, and my mother and two brothers. They all gave me a hug and put thruppences, or sixpences, in my hand. Mrs. Hagan held me by my shoulders and kissed me on the cheek and said, "Be a good wee girl for yer da and do what he tells ye, nye. Won't ye?"

As my father and I walked away from the small waving crowd, I kept turning around looking at my mother, hoping she would change her mind about sending me away. She didn't, and I knew deep down that she couldn't. We reached the bottom of our street, and before turning the corner, I looked back one last time. David and William were waving. My mother stood behind them with her head bent forward as though in prayer. My father gave my hand a gentle tug, and we turned the corner.

My mother and brothers were out of sight and I started to cry.

THREE

We headed up the Shankill Road and through tear-filled eyes the blurry image of Cave Hill loomed darkly on the horizon. The acrid smell of creosote was everywhere. Through veiled windows, I could see shadowy figures lighting coal fires to warm their damp, cold houses. Once the fire was lit, the kettle would be put on for a steaming hot cup of tea. But for my father and me there would be no such comfort. I felt terribly homesick already. Wiping tears from my eyes I looked up towards the hills and wondered where I would be sleeping that night.

A fine mist hung in the still air, soaking me through to the skin. I was cold, wet and shivering. Over and over I kept thinking, I want to go home, and now and then it slipped out of my mouth. Then my father would stop and hug me and say that everything was going to be all right and that before we knew it, we'd all be together again. Finally, the words slipped out one time too many and sternly he said, "Would ya stop yer gurnin', it's not doin' either of us any good!" The rebuke from my mild father might have provoked more tears but for the knowledge that he felt as bad as I did. I stopped crying.

We walked for a long time along stony roads that never seemed to end. In the country we passed other foot-weary people walking into Belfast to their job or to the shops, and exchanged nods and greetings. Now and again a car or a bus or a lorry filled with pigs or cows going to the slaughterhouse passed us. By the time we had walked six or seven miles, I felt that we had walked a hundred. My legs ached, and my feet were sore. The heels of my new mutton dummies were bright red from blisters that had burst and bled.

My father tried to distract me from my accumulating misery by making up stories. For a while we were soldiers on the way to war marching and chanting: "Left . . . left . . . we had a good home and we left . . . left . . ." If I had thought about what I was saying, I would have felt worse than I did, but in fact I began to enjoy the rhythm of the chant and the camaraderie of keeping in step with my marching father. He knew all about being a soldier, having spent ten years in the army. He spent three of those years in the British Army Special Forces in Burma, called Chindits. He never told me much about what he did in the jungle. I knew by the sadness in his eyes that it caused him grief even to think about that time. My brothers used to pester him to tell, but that look would come into his eyes and I would shush them.

But I must not think of my brothers.

"Left . . . left . . . we had a good home and we left . . . left . . ." On and on we marched. I tried to keep in step, which was, of course, impossible. No sooner had we finished one song then he'd start singing another. When I started to sniffle or lag behind, he broke into one of my favourites: "Not last night but the night before, three wee monkeys came to my door, one had whiskey, one had rum, and one had a pancake tied to his bum."

I found this very funny and asked, "Why would a monkey have a pancake tied to his bum?"

He'd just smile and say, "Ach, Cushla, darlin', its only a funny wee song to make children laugh."

I was christened Kathleen, but my father rarely called me that. He usually called me "Darlin" or "Cushla." "Cushla" comes from the Irish Gaelic word mo cuisle, pronounced macushla, which in English means "beat of my heart." Hearing him use it now was bittersweet, reminding me of home and also that we were together.

After walking almost ten hours, stopping to rest several times along the way, my stomach grumbled and my legs wobbled. My father pointed to the bottom of the hill.

"Look, Cushla, there's a farm down there." He reached into his pocket and brought out a few coins and said, "I've got nine pence in change. Let's see if the farmer'll sell us some buttermilk."

I could hardly wait. My legs seemed to respond with a life of their own to the idea of savouring delicious, salty-sweet buttermilk. The farmer was at the side of his house pumping water into a rusty, old bucket. He waved a friendly welcome as we approached the house. As it turned out he was indeed a generous fellow, and he let me drink as much buttermilk as I wanted. It was creamy and delicious.

My father gave me half of a wheaten farl smothered in treacle from a suitcase he had brought from home.

When we left, my mother had handed my father a well-worn brown leather suitcase. It contained three soda farls, three wheaten farls, a large crockery jam pot filled with sticky black treacle and a small glass jar filled with my mother's homemade butter.

It also contained my navy blue dress, two pairs of hand-knitted woollen knickers, a shirt and trousers, a clean pair of drawers for my father, two woollen cardigans, half a dozen hankies and my father's shaving kit.

Full and satisfied, my grumbling stomach calmed as I sat on a soft, golden mound of hay. In an instant my mind had retraced all the miles between here and Belfast, and I was back home with my kind, hard-working mother. Although we didn't have much money, she always kept us clean, and I couldn't remember ever being hungry. I thought of her sturdy and sustaining meals, sometimes just consisting of mashed or boiled potatoes with plenty of butter and soda bread, which she made every day on a large, cast-iron griddle. The butter came from cream we bought from Ned Green, the farmer who lived not far from our house on Nore Street. He kept about a dozen chickens, five or six pigs and two cows, and he had two greyhounds, which he raced on Friday and Saturday nights. My mother bought eggs, milk, cream and buttermilk from Ned. Quite often she would have to put them on "tick" and pay for them at the end of the week when she got her pay. Other times, if she had a shilling or two left over on a Friday, she would buy pigs' feet, fondly called "trotters," or sausages for a special treat. Every day she saved the peelings from turnips, carrots and unwanted leaves of cabbages for me to take in a bucket to Ned Green for his pigs.

Potato skins were saved for the fire. When she couldn't afford proper coal, she bought a bag of slack. Slack is coal dust and small bits of coal found at the bottom of the coal bag. My mother would set the fire before going to bed, light the slack and put the damp potato skins on top, which slowed the burning of the slack. In the middle of the night she would get up and scrape off the potato skins. The slack would ignite and warm the room for us getting up in the morning.

Mr. Green's pigs scared me, and so I brought my mind back to the butter, which I could still taste from my supper. Irish butter has a reputation all over the world for being of excellent quality, and my mother made the best. She saved butter-making for the times when her friends and neighbours came to visit. I loved this combination chore and social event. After sending me to buy the cream from Farmer Green, she put it in a large glass jar, making sure the top was screwed on tightly. Then she'd add salt, and while talking with friends, she sat and shook it. All the women took turns, and every so often the top of the jar was removed and any liquid that had separated was poured off. When the butter was ready, my mother patted it into a wooden box, separated in four one-pound sections, which she covered with a clean tea cloth and put out in the yard to set. When it was set, she turned the box upside down, removed the wooden sections, and wrapped the solidified butter in what she called "tishy" paper and stored them in the cupboard.

A burst of laughter from my father interrupted my thoughts and brought me back to the reality of my homelessness.

The sun was sinking fast behind the misty purple hills. Dark, elongated shadows from the tall elm trees threw a striped pattern onto the pale green rapeseed fields. The smell of burning peat, pungent and homey, hung in the cool twilight air. It wafted over to me from the farmhouse chimney, stinging my nose and saturating my mind with warm memories of home.

While my father and the talkative farmer shared an amusing yarn, I wondered where I was going to sleep that night. That question was soon answered.

I lay down on the newly mown hay, waiting for my father to finish his conversation, and fell asleep. I was so exhausted, I hadn't wakened when my father carried me to the back shed.

Early the next morning, I woke up in a nest of sweet-smelling, golden hay, wakened out of a sound sleep by the loud "cock-a-doodle-doo" of the farmer's boisterous rooster.

That was my first day away from my mother.

FOUR

For almost three weeks, we walked along dirt roads, crossing fields, climbing hills and sleeping in meadows. If we were lucky, we found an abandoned cottage, with a bit of roof still intact. Most of these cottages, when they were inhabited, had thatched roofs, but when deserted and without upkeep, the blustery winds in these rugged Irish hills scattered the straw back to the land from whence it came. Cottages such as these were few and far between. Usually when it rained we had to settle for a bridge to take shelter under for the night, and then I curled up against my father to keep warm and cry myself to sleep without him hearing.

Uncomfortable sitting on stones and shivering in the blackness underneath a bridge, I'd hear the far-off sound of a train whistle. Its anguished scream would disturb the silence and make me feel more desolate and lonely than ever.

My efforts to keep my misery to myself were not very successful, and my father eventually grew tired of finding ways to console me. I was getting tired of tears myself, and they weren't helping, so I made up my mind to stop crying. This resolution was harder to carry out than I expected, but the effort made my father brighten up, and over time, so did I.

We didn't only walk. We also searched out every factory, foundry, mill and any other place that we thought might have work. There was nothing, and with just two pounds left and all our food gone, we were hungry and discouraged.

We reached the outskirts of a place called Ballymacruise, on the northeast coast of the Irish Sea, on the border between Ulster and the Irish Republic.

It was blustery and cold walking this close to the sea, and when the icy rain lashed my face, it felt like a thousand little needles piercing my skin. My coat wasn't much protection from the cold, biting wind, so I walked close behind my father, trying to stay out of the wind as much as I could.

Following a low stone wall, we walked along the deserted seafront. Squinting through the heavy mist swirling over the sea, I could just make out the faint outline of a lighthouse, its ghostly beacon flashing through the rain every few seconds. Totally mesmerized by the light, I was caught off guard when a deluge of freezing salt water crashed up over the wall covering me and nearly taking my breath away. My father opened his trench coat and wrapped me in it close to him, but I couldn't breathe and my legs were wet, stinging and bright red. This physical misery called forth every single tear I had been repressing, on account of homesickness, and I felt I had simply moved beyond consolation.

However, my father turned away from the sea and shuffled me up over a hill to the other side of the hill where the wind died down and the lashing rain became fine drizzle.

Gulping the misty air thankfully, I emerged from my father's coat. Looking up at the heavy, grey sky, the first thing I noticed was a spiralling ribbon of black smoke rising from behind a row of trees.

"Daddy, look over there, what could that be?"

Since we had no particular destination in mind, we investigated.

Walking through a clearing in the trees we saw men, women and children throwing whatever they could find onto a giant bonfire—rubber tires, rags, branches of trees and broken pieces of furniture were hurled into the flames. Two scruffy looking men lifted a sofa over their heads and tossed it in. I was spellbound for the moment. Even more wonderful than the strange and surreal scene was the heat from the fire. I wanted to get closer, but we stayed back.

At first, no one noticed us, but after about five minutes, over the laughing and shouting and the crackling of the fire, a man's deep voice bellowed, "Hey, you, take yourself off . . . you're not welcome here!"

We both by this time had realized that we had come upon a band of gypsies. "Y'know luv," my father said, "I think the best thing for us would be to turn on our heels and run. But then, bein' soakin' wet and hungry an' all, maybe we'll just havta take a chance and ask them if we kin stay for a couple o' days. Would that suit you, luv?"

It was common knowledge that gypsies stole children and performed a whole range of other unsavoury deeds. However, the heat from the fire and my father's nearness prevailed over any reluctance I felt on account of what were probably old wives' tales. I shrugged my shoulders. "All right."

My father shouted back, "Show yourself, whoever said that. I'd like to see who I'm talkin' to."

The man's voice shouted another question, but still he did not show himself. "Yer not a peeler are ya?"

"No, I'm not the police, but I'd like to talk to whoever's in charge. Would that happen to be you?"

By now, the laughter and shouting had died down and everyone was listening. Only the roaring fire crackled and spit. The crowd parted for a stocky, dirty man, large and powerfully built, with steel grey hair, dark eyes and a very dirty face. A soot-smudged, sweat-stained undershirt stretched over his ample belly. The man frightened me, and I clasped my father's hand tightly. I averted my eyes downward to the grass where little shamrocks and tiny daisies had been crushed under my feet as I stood watching the fire.

With an annoyed look on his grimy face, the man strode up to us and came to an abrupt halt. My father held out his hand in a gesture of friendship, which was ignored by the gypsy. The gypsy's insult was in turn ignored by my father, who spoke clearly and mildly.

"M'name's James McKenna and this is m'daughter Kathleen. I left Belfast over a fortnight ago in search of work. We're hungry, cold and tired. D'ya think y'could give us some food and shelter for a couple a days till we have a wee bit of a rest?"

The frowning man didn't say anything. He just stood there looking suspiciously up at my father and down to me as if trying to figure out what we were up to. When he finally opened his mouth to speak, drops of spittle drizzled down his chin, propelled through rotten, brown-stained teeth.

"So we know what you want from us, but what makes y'think you'd be welcome here? Y'mustn't have any money, or y'wouldn't be wantin' t'stay with the likes of us now, would ya? So how are ya goin' t'pay fer any food and lodgin' if, out of the goodness of our hearts, we decide to let y'stay?"

"I'm willin' to work for whativer y'give us," my father replied, maintaining rigid eye contact. "I'm a hard worker, and I'm good at fixin' things."

The crowd of people laughed, even their spokesman. "Well, we're not too worried about fixin' things around here, but we kin put ye t'work, for sure. Whether you'll like the kinda work, is another thing entirely."

My father was slightly taller than the older, swarthy man, but he was of a slighter build and looked much more respectable.

After a pause the old gypsy continued, "D'ya have a problem with doing things that are not exactly within the law?"

To my surprise, my father only shrugged. "Well, nye that would depend on the circumstances. I'll take no part in anything that would hurt somebody."

"It might mean stealin' food and the like."

"Well, it wouldn't be the first time I've had to do that now, so no, that wouldn't bother me."

This was even more startling, but there was no question of asking what he meant. I didn't really want to know.

"Fair enough then," the gypsy man answered, "I bid you and your daughter welcome but, mind you, you'll work for whativer you get."

Then he said his name was Archie Mallon, and he thrust out a very dirty hand, which my father shook.

Archie Mallon and his wife Nora lived in an abandoned farmhouse with their grandson Stevie. It would soon be winter, and gypsies always tried to find somewhere to squat for two or three months during the winter. When the weather improved, they resumed their nomad's life, wearing out their welcome wherever they went.

Stevie was about my age, but had a mean look about him, and I disliked him instantly. Nora seemed nice enough, though. She was a small, thin woman who wore her steel grey hair knotted so tightly on the top of her head that her dark-brown eyes looked slanted and oriental. When she smiled I saw that she had no teeth.

My father noticed that, too, and being the kind of person who could not let the opportunity pass to make a witty remark, bent down and whispered in my ear, "That wee woman hasn't a bar in her grate."

Nora led us over to our new abode. It looked like a covered wooden horse cart. My father told me it was called a caravan. An empty wooden whiskey barrel compensated for a missing wheel, and there were no steps up to the front door. Nora pointed to the trees behind the caravan. "Over yonder, you'll find a wee wooden crate. Bring it over, an' it'll do nicely for a step for yer wee lass."

My father retrieved the crate and placed it in front of the door. The ground underneath was uneven, and the crate wobbled and teetered when I stood on it.

Nora went up first, then my father. When he reached the opening, he turned and grasped my hand to steady me on the way up. We stepped through the dark yawning mouth of the caravan. There was no actual door, but hanging on a nail attached to the right-hand side of the frame was a ragged grey army blanket. Nora pointed to another nail on the other side of the frame and said that the blanket could be stretched across. That was our front door.

A wooden shelf ran along each side of the caravan; Nora said that she would get us two ticks and two blankets to put on top of them. I asked her what she meant by a tick. The only time I heard that word used was when my mother couldn't pay for something right away and she would put it on "tick" until payday at the end of the week.

Nora laughed and said, "It's a wee mattress filled with straw, sheep's wool and feathers that'll put a bit o' paddin' between yer wee skinny bones and that wooden shelf you'll be lyin' on."

At the back of the caravan, between the two shelves, was a vegetable crate stood on its end. On top was a candle stuck in a broken cup. The caravan was very sparse and lacked every single thing that a home should have, but at least we'd have a roof over our heads that night and we wouldn't be sleeping in a field in the rain.

Nora was old in her appearance, but she demonstrated vitality by jumping down from the caravan. She looked back at us and said, "Ill be back in a wee minute, so make yerselves at home."

My father took a match from his trouser pocket and lit the candle, then walked back to the blanket and covered the front door. He bent over and looked into my face, "Well, luv, waddya think?"

Rather than lie, I walked over and hugged him. "I'll feel a bit better when I git outta these wet clothes," I said, trying to sound optimistic. Alarmed, he pushed me away from him and held me at arms' length. "Oh, my God, luv, you've just reminded me I left the case outside. I hope it's still there." He disappeared and in a few seconds pushed the suitcase through the army blanket. "Whew! Thank God. I don't mean to be ungracious to our hosts, thinkin' that somebody might have made off with it, but they are gypsies after all." We both chuckled, but quietly.

"Well, luv, while you're changing into some dry clothes, I'm goin' t'take a wee walk outside and see what this place is about."

I shivered getting out of my dripping clothes, but even wearing dry ones, I was still cold enough to cup my hands around the flame of the candle in the cup.

Nora came back with the ticks, which looked like two overstuffed flour bags, and two worn, grey woollen blankets, which she put on the shelves, plus a very dented pot that she told me to put under my bed.

Parting the army blanket to leave she said, "I'll bid good night t'y'now, sleep well. Come over to the big house in the mornin' and get yer breakfast. I'll send some supper over for you and yer da."

A short while later, a small, plump woman wearing a food-spattered apron stumbled up the rickety steps, nearly spilling the contents of the bowls she carried in each hand onto the floor as well as herself. A spoon fell out of one bowl and bounced onto the floor in front of her. In her loud coarse voice she swore, "Jezez Christ, I nearly crigged me arse gittin' up that friggin' wobbly step." Licking her fingers, she handed me a steaming bowl, which smelled deliciously like mutton stew.

She put a bigger bowl of the same on the table by the candle for my father. She went back to where the spoon had fallen, picked it up and wiped it up on her dirty apron, and handed it to me. She smiled down at me exposing large brown-stained teeth and introduced herself, "Annie Sloan's m'name, and what's yours, luv?" I told her. She said, "Well, it's nice t'meet ye, Kathleen, nye you git that stew inta ya. By the looks of ya, y'need some meat on them bones."

Annie was an ugly woman. That was the only appropriate word I could think of to describe her. At first glance, my eyes were drawn to the focal point of her face—her two front teeth. They were large and stuck out, pressing into her lower lip making a permanent impression. She had several large fleshy moles on her face with hair growing out of them. Her eyes were slightly crossed, and she looked like she was actually talking to someone behind me, but I was alone in the caravan. Annie was ugly, but she wasn't scary, and I was inclined to like her. She bade me good night and told me to enjoy my supper. As she parted the blanket to leave, she cursed and mumbled something about breaking her friggin' neck on the step. She shouted to my father in her coarse, loud voice to come and eat his supper before it got cold.

Within a minute he was sitting on the bed opposite me. He said, with a mischievous look in his eye, "That wee woman Annie's no oil paintin'. She could turn milk sour just by lookin' at it. But, God help 'er, she has a kind heart."

I laughed and nodded in agreement and continued slurping the hot mutton stew. It was the first hot meal we'd had in days, and we both agreed that nothing ever before had tasted so delicious.

In the confines of the small, dark caravan, alone with my father and under very unusual circumstances, I felt secure for the first time in weeks. The comfortable feeling of a full belly and a dry bed lulled me into feeling content. Snuggling under the blanket I closed my eyes and murmured a wistful, "Goodnight, Daddy." He replied, "Goodnight, luv." But before drifting off to a dream world of gypsies and bonfires, I heard scratching and scurrying above my head. Too tired to worry about anything, I convinced myself it was only my imagination.

Later on I discovered that we shared our gypsy caravan with rats that had nested behind the loose ribs of the ceiling.

Most of the little I knew about gypsies came from my mother and the neighbour women, who told us to run and hide when we saw gypsies because they stole children and could put a spell on you by giving you the evil eye. They joked about the evil eye, but when gypsies came around the door selling little tin cups and pots, most people bought at least a cup to ward off the possibility of a curse. Many of my mother's friends considered it bad luck to turn a gypsy away without buying something. Half joking, my mother would say that gypsies would steal the eye out of your head and put in a soldier's button.

When my father and I left our home in Belfast, my mother told me to look on this journey with my father as an adventure. I didn't know that it would mean becoming a gypsy.

FIVE

First thing next morning I looked over to my father's bed. He was still asleep and snoring. I stared up at the bits of string and straw hanging from the roof of the caravan, wondering what the day would bring. The gypsies were already about their morning business. I heard clanging, then water being splashed onto the ground.

My father finally woke up, got out of bed and put on his trousers. He said that he would be back in a wee minute and that he had to see a man about a dog. I knew what he meant; he wouldn't have used the po' under my bed, especially in front of me. He came back in a very short while, rubbing his hands together.

"Brrr, it would skin ye out there."

He sat back down on his bed and rolled and lit a cigarette, and drew in a long, satisfying drag. He usually smoked Woodbines. Coffin nails he called them, but now he had to roll his own.

Smoke flowed from his nostrils and mouth."Top o' the mornin', darlin', and what might y' be thinkin' about?"

I said that I was wondering what all the clanging and splashing was. He smiled, "Aye, well nye, that's the night's pish being emptied. It certainly wouldn't be wash basins, cuz these fellahs don't seem too bothered about washin' themselves."

I had only two dresses with me. One that I wore everyday, and my good navy wool dress for special occasions. I had brought one heavy woollen cardigan for outdoors and one finely knit one, which I slept in, so I never had to wonder what to wear. I put on a clean pair of knickers, although I didn't really like wearing the woollen knickers my mother knitted for me because they made my backside itch.

Getting out of bed that first morning, I stood shivering, putting my clothes on. We were close to the sea, and the early morning mist made them cold and damp. I resolved that I would take my clothes into bed with me and get dressed under the covers for as long as we were there.

We ventured out of our caravan and looked around at the gypsy camp. There were seven caravans in a circle, and at the top of the circle was a large, grey stone farmhouse that looked in bad need of repair and too falling-down to be habitable. Cardboard covered broken windows, and a gaping hole in the roof had been patched with muck and straw. The front door was completely covered with a thick vine. As we walked to the house, scraggly, sleepy people emerged from their caravans. They stared at us with scowling, unfriendly looks on their dirty faces.

The bonfire was still smoldering and giving off welcoming heat. I wanted to stop and warm myself for a minute or two, but my father put his arm around my shoulder and propelled me forward. "Come on, luv, you'll be warmer when y' git somethin' t'eat."

I didn't protest because I was as hungry as I was cold.

As we approached the farmhouse door, Nora parted the thick curtain of vines so thick no wind or rain could penetrate them. She stood in the threshold holding them back for us to go through. Hers was the first friendly face we saw, and she greeted us with a wide toothless grin.

"Good mornin' to ya. Did yez sleep all right?"

My father assured her that we did and thanked her once again. Nora put a steaming cup of tea into his hands, and slurping noisily, he left the farmhouse and joined a group of men standing around the dying bonfire.

"Well, chile, wud you like some bread and warm milk?"

Since my stomach had been grumbling since I woke up, that sounded wonderful to me.

Putting her arm around my shoulder, she said, "Go on over an' warm yourself by the fire while I put yer breakfast out."

I walked through the cluttered room and turned my back to the fire. It was the only room still intact. It was large with a fireplace in the middle of the back wall. In the soot-covered fireplace behind me, a bubbling, steaming cauldron was suspended over hot glowing embers by a long chain. The chain was attached to an iron bracket, which was secured to the side of the fireplace. I looked into the pot to see what Nora was cooking.

Two blood-filled, bulging eyes looked back at me, faded and bobbing loosely in their sockets. It was a skinned sheep's head with half its flesh boiled away. Pale shredded lips flapped loosely in the bubbles exposing flat yellow teeth. Shocked at the grisly sight before me, I shut my eyes, clamped my hand over my mouth to keep from crying out and turned away quickly.

Trying to take my mind off the contents of the boiling pot, I looked around the room. It was very untidy and filled with a lot of rubbish. Archie was still asleep on a worn, stained mattress on the floor in the corner. Nora waved her hand in his direction

"Niver bother your head about him, he'll be there till dinnertime."

She told me to sit down at a cluttered table where colourful cards were spread out in a circle. Spilling out from a black leather drawstring pouch beside the cards were little flat stones with strange marks on them. She picked up the cards and pushed them to the back of the table by the wall and scooped up the stones and put them in the pouch. Pulling the drawstring tight she put the little bag in a crockery jar and pushed it away beside the cards.

Having cleared the table, she placed before me a blue and white chipped bowl filled with bread broken into small pieces. She poured warm milk over it and reached up to a shelf over the kitchen table and retrieved another crockery pot. She handed me a spoon and told me to use the sugar sparingly as that was all they had left. "Go on nye, you git that inta ya," she ordered kindly.

I ate quickly; it was sweet and warm, and I finally stopped shivering.

"There yar nye, wasn't that luvly?" asked Nora. "Nye, you be a good girl and go and find some childer to play with. There's plenty o' them around here."

At the vines, I turned and asked, "Can I have a look at yer wee cards on the table? I'd like to see the pictures on them."

Nora shook her head. "No, luv, ye can't. Them's me tarot cards, and nobody but me can touch them."

I hesitated and tried again. "Well, then, can I have a look at yer funny wee stones."

Nora shook her head again. "I'm sorry, luv, but ye can't touch them either. Them's me runes, and they're very special. Ye can't touch these special things 'cause they've got me energy on them. If you were ta touch them, they'd lose their magic, and I'd have t' start and put me energy inta them all over again, and I can only do that once a month when the moon's full."

This was tantalizing, and I persisted. I asked her if she could show me how the cards and stones worked.

"I will, luv, but the magic works better in the dark. It's more potent when the sun's gone down. One of these nights I'll tell yer fortune, but it'll cost ye a sixpence. The magic's stronger if silver crosses me palm."

I would have to be satisfied with that, so I thanked her for breakfast and pushed my way out through the heavy vines.

The first boy I met was Stevie Mallon. He was a large, lumbering, pale boy with short-cropped, light brown hair. It looked like someone had cut it with blunt scissors wearing a blindfold. His eyes were small and spaced far apart on his head, and if he'd had pointy ears and a curly tail you could've mistaken him for a pig. He came over when he saw me.

"Wera you from?" he asked, squinting at me through his piggy eyes.

I answered shyly, "Belfast."

Proudly he said, "M' da's in Belfast. He's in the Crumlin Road Jail."

I was shocked. I thought to myself, if my father was in jail, I certainly wouldn't tell anybody. Especially the Crumlin Road Jail. You had to be a real criminal to be put in there. I had never known anyone before whose father was in jail, or anyone else for that matter. Absentmindedly burying his finger up his nose, Stevie continued.

"I'm stayin' with m' granny and granda till m' da gets out. Then me and him are goin' to America."

If my father had been here and seen what he was doing, he'd have said, "Hey, boyo, stop pickin' yer willick, yer head'll cave in." But I settled for trying to ignore what he was doing and asked him where his mother was.

Rolling the nugget he extracted from his nose into a ball and flicking it onto the ground between us, he said, "Ach, m' ma ran off. I haven't seen 'er since I was six, and now I'm thirteen so I don't 'member 'er much."

I also didn't know anyone whose mother had run away, though it did cross my mind that having a child like Stevie would be a mighty temptation. I didn't feel comfortable around Stevie, so as he kept up a one-sided conversation, I kept a close watch on my father, who was talking to two men just the other side of the bonfire. There was a shifty, evil look in Stevie's little piggy eyes, which suggested to me that he wasn't to be trusted.

Stevie then told me that we would be going "shappin." Gypsy children had specific tasks that they had to do as well as all the adults. "Shappin" meant that the women and children got vegetables any way they could, either by stealing them from a farmer's field or by going into town and nicking them from the market or an open stall outside a shop.

In any event, we didn't go "shappin" that day. Instead, Nora took me just over the hill to where creamy white mushrooms dotted the hillside. She told me to fold my dress up to make it into a basket and fill it. After filling my scooped-up dress with mushrooms, Nora picked through them, discarding any she thought unsuitable, and we headed back to camp. On the way she told me that tomorrow morning, bright and early, we would go down to the seashore to gather cockles, crabs and whelks. She said that after picking the wee snail out of the whelk shell with a safety pin and twisting the nippers off the wee crabs, she would make a big pot of soup with them. Smacking her lips as she described the soup, Nora smiled a wide toothless grin.

"Ach, it's lovely, so it is. You'll enjoy it."

At the camp, other women and children were emptying their less honestly obtained offerings into a big wooden barrel that sat outside the farmhouse. Nora smiled at the variety of contributions that everyone had managed to steal, and rubbing her hands together, she exclaimed, "We'll be eatin' good the night."

I asked her where my father was, and she told me that he had gone with the men to do their "shappin." Five men had set off up the big hill at the back of the camp to steal a sheep, which they would skin and gut on the spot. They'd bring back the ready carcass, the hide and some of the other edible bits.

When my father and the men returned with what would be supper for a week, he told me that he did not like what he had just done and would have to find some other way to work for our keep. This made more sense to me than his earlier indifference to breaking the law.

All my life my mother had taught me that stealing was wrong, and now living with the gypsies, it seemed likely I would have to steal to survive. I wondered if she would refuse under the circumstances. She had quoted the Ten Commandments to me often enough. Sometimes she would test my knowledge.

"Kathleen, what is the Fifth Commandment?"

"Honour thy father and thy mother."

"Good girl," she would say. "Always remember that. What is the Eighth Commandment?"

"Thou shalt not steal."

Some days she would test me on all ten. She knew the Bible back to front. She could recite all the books of the Old and New Testaments at lightning speed without faltering. I hoped she wouldn't be disappointed in me when she found out what I had to do in order to survive.

I loved my mother; she was hard-working and generous, and thinking about her made me melancholy. I felt like indulging myself, so I deliberately imagined her standing over the gas stove on a Monday morning, wiping sweat from her eyes as she boiled water to fill the big washtub in the yard. She carried heavy loads of washing to the back shed and placed them in the washtub on the wooden stand. She scrubbed until her hands were red from the strong washing soda. When she finished, she put the clothes, towels and bedsheets through the mangle and turned the handle. This required strength, so my mother did that part, and I caught the washing at the other side and put it into another washtub filled with cold water for rinsing. After rinsing, the clothes were put through the mangle again, and I put them in a basket ready for my mother to hang on the line.

I didn't really appreciate all the hard work that my mother did for me, but that first day with the gypsies made me realize just how lucky I was to have loving parents and a stable, comfortable home, no matter how humble it was. In a few months these unfortunate people would be moving again, not knowing where their next meal would come from. I expected I would be back in Belfast with my mother, and oh, how happy to help her with the laundry.

That evening for supper, we ate our fill of mutton stew again, and it was soon time for me to go to bed. My father tucked me in and as usual sang me some songs and told me stories. He started off with:

"There was a wee man and you called him Dan,
 He washed his face in a fryin' pan,
He combed his hair with a donkey's tail,
And he scratched his belly with his big toe nail."

That was followed by:

"There was a wee man and you called him Sam,
And he had no eyes for to see,
He had no teeth for to eat his oatcake,
So he had to leave his oatcake be."

Then he sang one of my mother's songs:

"My Aunt Jane, she called me in,
She gave me tea out of her wee tin,
Half a bap and sugar on the top,
And three black lumps out of her wee shop."

My mother's version of the second verse was:

"My Aunt Jane, she's awful smart,
She baked her rings in an apple tart,
Candy apples and hard green pears,
And conversation lozengers."

My father's version made me laugh, as it was intended to:

"My Aunt Jane, she's awful smart,
She ate some beans, then she'd fart,
Candy apples and hard green pears,
She shite herself runnin' up the stairs."

We both laughed, and as if we were at home, he stuck his finger out at me and told me to pull it. I did, of course. He lifted his leg and farted loud enough for anyone standing near the caravan to hear and exclaimed, "Ach, Kathleen, catch yerself on girl, yer stinkin' up the caravan!"

"Daddy, y'know it was you!"

We laughed, and then he settled me down by stroking my brow. Then we knelt side by side and said our prayers, asking God to bless my mother and my two brothers and keep them safe till we were all together again. I asked God to help find my father a good job. We said "Amen" together, and he kissed me gently on the cheek and whispered, "Goodnight, luv, I'll see ya in the mornin'."

SIX

It was almost the end of October, and every day was the same as the one before. I was awakened each morning by a clanging of the gypsies emptying the contents of their chamberpots from the night before. The foul steaming matter made a splattering noise when it hit the ground. Sometimes the sound made me put off going to Nora's for breakfast.

Every day, my father would go off with the men to steal the day's provisions. We intended to stay only a few days, but at the end of three weeks, we seemed no closer to going home. My father remained optimistic, firmly believing that something good would happen any day.

My father decided that we should go into town to have a wee look around and find a post office. He had a stack of letters that he had written to my mother, and he wanted to post them. He winked at me, and with an impish look in his eye he said, "Maybe we'll even try to nick some vegetables ourselves while we're at it, since we've plundered oul farmer Donnelly's fields bare."

We went over to tell Nora what we were planning to do. Nora was standing in front of the fireplace holding something that looked like a brush on a long pole high above her head, but instead of bristles on the end, there was an iron weight. She said, as she thumped down the iron weight on the scuffed floor, "This oul dirt floor has to be beetled every day. If ya don't do it, the dirt gits in yer shoes, makin' yer feet blacker than iver."

When we told Nora that we were going into town for the day; she looked at us suspiciously, "Yer not thinkin' of buggerin' off nye, are ye?"

We assured her that we would be back for supper and left quickly.

I felt close to my father when I had him to myself. As we walked down the hill towards town, his velvety voice echoed over the hills as he sang, "If I were a black bird I'd whistle and sing, I'd follow the ship that my true love sailed in." He stopped singing to point to the "Welcome to Ballymacruise" sign and said, "Well, darlin', let's see what kind o' mischief we kin git up to here."

It was a lovely little town with rows of clean, whitewashed cottages. Some still had flowerpots filled with white and purple alyssum, dainty primroses and colourful, fragrant sweet william. Blocks of black peat were stacked at the side of most cottages in readiness for the cold, damp winter weather. Ballymacruise would be miserably cold being so close to the sea, blasted by fierce winds and sudden squalls.

But that day in Ballymacruise the sun was shining. It had rained in the night and a scattering of black clouds still lolled puffy and low over the sea. We had a good look around the town and finally found a post office. My father had written a letter to my mother every day. I had lost track of time, but the thick bundle of letters he carried told me we had been with the gypsies longer than I had wanted to be. They were too thick to put in an envelope so he just rolled them up, tied them with a string and posted them without a return address. We didn't have one.

Walking back towards the gypsy camp, we walked through the marketplace. As we passed, people in the busy market turned away from us, and I heard them muttering something about dirty gypsies and telling their children not to look us in the eye because it was bad luck. I was a shocked when I realized they thought that my father and I were gypsies, and I never got used to it.

Because we spent most of the day in town, my father couldn't go stealing with the men, but he knew that he couldn't go back to the camp empty-handed. He hadn't been joking about nicking something to take back.

The market was the busiest place in Ballymacruise. There was a sign on the front gate surrounding the courthouse, indicating that it was held on the grounds every Saturday until the end of November. The gates were open and there were stalls filled with all kinds of fruits and vegetables—more apples, oranges, bananas and melons than I had ever seen in my life. Stall after stall of clothes, boots, shoes and rugs captured my attention. Attractive, colourful rows of flowers enticed people to come and be part of the cheerful hubbub of Saturday morning market-day shopping.

Not everything was pleasant. Shanks of bloody red meat impaled on hooks dangled from the wooden supports on the butchers' stands. Dead chickens and rabbits, their heads lolling in the wind, were hung upside down by their feet. Even a quick passing glance at their glassy staring eyes gave me a queasy feeling in my stomach and reminded me of the sheep's head in Nora's kettle.

We walked around the market several times until my father finally got up enough nerve to try his hand at stealing in a public place. He chose a vegetable stall whose owner was talking seriously to an elderly couple and not paying too much attention to what was going on behind him. My father looked at me, took a deep breath, exhaled slowly and said, "Well, its nye or niver," and snatched the biggest turnip he could see and stuck it under his arm.

Grasping my hand firmly, he said. "Let's get outta here quick," and yanked me away from the vegetable stall.

We had not got far before a man shouted, "Oy there, mate! Whaddya think yer doin? Come back here with that turnip!"

My father glanced over his shoulder and exclaimed, "Oh, Jezez, he's blowin' 'is bloody whistle. We'll have every peeler in town after us."

We ran up the street, my father holding onto the turnip in the crook of his left arm, like a wrestler with his opponent in a headlock, and trailing me along with the other. We raced to the top of the street, turned a corner and kept on running, until halfway down the street we found a house almost hidden by high brick walls with its garden gate left open. We dashed in and closed the gate. We pressed our backs up against the brick wall, standing rigid and silent until we could catch our breath. After a minute, my father looked down at me and asked, "Are ye all right, luv?"

Still out of breath and too frightened to speak, I nodded. He pushed the stolen turnip into my hands and whispered, "I've got an idea, luv, that just might git us outta here without gittin' caught."

He turned his back to me, bent forward and told me to stick the turnip up his coat, in between his shoulder blades. He pulled his hat down over his ears and remaining bent over he limped and walked around the yard pretending to be a hunchback. I stared at him in disbelief. I shook my head and laughed.

"Oh! Daddy, you're a head case."

He twisted his mouth and crinkled his nose and said, "I might look like an ejit, but it just might git us outta the mess we've got ourselves into."

Taking hold of my hand we walked through the gate and up the street, away from the market. I kept looking at him out of the corner of my eye, feeling ridiculous. At the sound of running feet he pushed me into a doorway that had been left open and told me to be as quiet as a wee mouse and not to be scared, everything would be all right.

From my hiding place I could see the dark shadow of a lanky policeman hurtle past us. He came to an abrupt halt a few steps ahead of my father and walked back to speak to him. I held my breath and pressed myself further into the darkest corner of the doorway. I couldn't see either of them clearly, but I could see the policeman's shadow bent over and he appeared to be looking directly into my father's face.

"Excuse me," I heard him say to my father breathlessly but politely, "Have you seen a gypsy fella and a young gypsy girl runnin' up this street?"

Making his voice sound weak and croaky, my father answered calmly and politely, "No, sir, nobody attal."

The policeman thanked him and was about to leave when he hesitated, looked at the unusual character in front of him and asked, "And who might you be, sir? I haven't seen you around here before."

Avoiding eye contact, my father continued in his croaky voice, "I'm just here for the day, constable, enjoyin' the seaside."

The policeman accepted his response, tipped his cap and said, "Well, see and enjoy yourself, sir," and ran back the way he came.

We breathed a sigh of relief and when we were certain that the policeman had truly been hoodwinked, we headed out of town. My father waited until we were well past the busy part of town before he took the turnip out from under his coat. He tossed it in the air, and I laughed so hard that I peed my woollen knickers. I took them off and my father stuck them in his pocket. He told me to rinse them out when we got back to the gypsy camp, which meant that I would be without knickers for a couple of days. My other pair had been rinsed out a day or so ago and still weren't dry.

We took our time going back. I felt happy. We stopped to read a notice tacked to a telegraph post. As he read it an odd expression came on his face.

"Cushla, darlin', " he said excitedly. "I might have just found a way to make a few quid and get us back home."

The notice advertised a boxing match. My father had boxed in the army to keep in shape and help pass the time when he wasn't on active duty. His brother Pat had been an all-Ireland boxing champion in the 1940s, and my father was his sparring partner when he was in Belfast.

His face suddenly brightened and his step seemed lighter. I, too, felt exhilarated, although my happiness was already tempered by the thought of him getting hurt.

At the bottom of the poster, in large black letters, was the name Jack Rooney, and underneath was the address of a boxing club. My father ripped off the poster, rolled it up and stuck it under his arm. We hid the turnip behind a fence post and covered it with grass intending to pick it up on our way back. No idea of where we were going, we headed back to town.

Avoiding the marketplace, we kept to the back streets. Finding the boxing club wasn't easy and people weren't helpful. When my father asked for directions, they would turn away without saying a word.

It took us a while, but we finally found the club, a converted warehouse with a large front door. My father had to press hard on the rusty iron latch and push the rickety front door open. Inside I crinkled up my nose at the overpowering smell of stale sweat mixed with some other smell that I couldn't identify. It was dark inside with nobody in sight, except for the light coming from the open door behind us and two windows placed high on opposite walls. There was a raised square platform with posts on each corner. Ropes were attached to them, enclosing the platform. I thought to myself, that must be the boxin' ring, and wondered why they called it a ring when it was obviously a square. I imagined my father standing in the middle with his two hands in the air after winning.

So lost was I in this daydream that I was startled by a tall, burly fellow with a bald head and a full black mustache who suddenly crept out of the shadows. My father was making his way around the ring when the man placed himself so as to obstruct his progress.

"Hold on there, boyo, who are ya and where do ya think you're goin'?"

"I'm lookin' for Jack Rooney," my father answered boldly, unrolling the poster.

"And what makes ya think that Jack Rooney wants to see you?" the bald man asked gruffly.

My father unrolled the poster with a small flourish. "He'll want to see me all right, 'cause I kin knock out any man named on this boxin' poster!"

A small man with red hair appeared from behind the boxing ring.

"What makes ya think you're so tough, gypo?"

My father strode over to the small man until he towered over him. "First of all, mate, I'm no gypsy, I'm lookin' for work and haven't had much luck." Then, realizing that a sharp tongue would get him nowhere, he moderated his voice and introduced himself. "M'name's Jim McKenna and this is m'wee daughter Kathleen. We've walked all the way from Belfast." He went on to tell him how we were tired and hungry and out of money and had joined the gypsies out of desperation.

Jack Rooney, for the little man he was, sized up my father. "All right, so you've got a sad story to tell, but what makes ya think ya kin fight?"

"D' ya know a boxer called Pat McKenna?" Knowing that anyone in the boxing business in Ireland would, he didn't wait for an answer. "Well, he's m' brother, and when he was fightin' professionally and came home to visit his family in Belfast, I was his sparrin' partner."

"Ach, aye, I know 'im well and that fellah was one hell of a fighter. If you're half as good as him, you'll do all right."

He told my father to bring his gear and come back the following Friday night and that he would be fightin' somebody called Abe McDuff. My father told him that he had no gear. Mr. Rooney shook his head impatiently and told him that he could borrow boxing gloves belonging to the club. They shook hands and Mr. Rooney grunted goodbye and said, "See ya Friday, gypo."

My father left the boxing club both satisfied and annoyed, but the look on his face was one of hope. With a twinkle in his eye, he said, "Well, ma girl, we mustn't forget that turnip. This might be the last time I'll have to nick anything."

SEVEN

It took us a half an hour to walk back. The grass seemed greener, the clouds didn't seem as dark and my father's voice was even more lilting than usual.

Walking lightheartedly back to the gypsy camp, we tossed the stolen turnip back and forth to each other. The turnip was large and heavy, and many times it slipped through my fingers and crashed onto the gravel road. Its once smooth skin became pocked and scraped.

When we arrived at the gypsy camp, my father said, "I've got t' talk ta Archie for a wee minute, luv, you go on ahead. I won't be long."

When I reached the caravan I rolled the scarred turnip in through the army blanket. I desperately needed to pee. I checked to see if there was anybody around, and then I went behind the back corner of our caravan. But as I lifted my dress and squatted down, Stevie Mallon was suddenly behind me.

He pointed at my bare backside and as loud as he could, he yelled, "Hey, girl, where's your knickers?"

He laughed and kept shouting and pointing at me and soon there was a crowd of boys about Stevie's age and a couple of girls all laughing at me. I stood up and tried to run, but Stevie grabbed my hand and swept me up in his arms and started swinging me around and around. The wind blew my dress up over my backside and everyone in that circle had a good look at everything a young girl likes to keep private.

They began chanting, "Kathleen's got no knickers on," over and over. Finally Stevie put me down, and I was so dizzy I fell forward on my hands and knees. Stevie pulled my dress up and walloped me hard on the bare backside. Everyone laughed and cheered when they heard the loud stinging smack. I felt unbearably humiliated and helpless. Their laughter stripped away every ounce of my dignity. I hated them all, and my head was spinning, my bladder bursting, and I couldn't even stand up to fight back.

Then a boy behind me shouted, "Stevie, hold her dress up so we can all have a go at smackin' 'er backside!"

At this point I was so terrified and crying so loudly that I didn't realize for a moment that the taunting gypsy children had suddenly become quiet. I looked around. My father was holding Stevie suspended in mid-air by the collar of his thread-bare coat. Stevie was shouting that he didn't mean any harm and that he was just havin' a wee bit o' fun.

I heard my father growl through clenched teeth, "You'll not be havin' fun with my wee girl. I'm takin' you to your granda, and I'll let him deal with ya." Gripping Stevie's arm firmly, my father marched him, none too gently, to the farmhouse.

I was relieved in one way, but I still needed desperately to pee, so I found a more secluded spot away from the caravan behind a tree. I was very thankful that I hadn't peed myself when Stevie was spinning me around. That humiliation would have been unbearable. The children of the camp despised me enough already.

I went back to the caravan, still feeling nervous and embarrased. I climbed the rickety steps holding the bottom of my dress tightly around my thighs. My bare backside had had enough exposure for one day.

My father came in right behind me and took me in his arms and sat down on his bed with me on his knee while I had a good cry. Cradled in my father's arms I could hear Stevie Mallon yelling his head off in the distance. That was one consolation. Both Archie and Nora were shouting, but Stevie was so loud, I couldn't make out what they were saying. When I finally stopped crying myself, I asked my father when my knickers would be dry. My father told me that when I got up in the morning I would have dry knickers to wear.

That night he gathered up the two pairs of damp knickers and took them over to Nora to dry them by the fire.

Stevie, for the most part, ignored me after that day, but the look in his eyes told me that he hated me. Sometimes when he thought that no one was looking he would spit at my feet when I passed him. I ignored him. I was still afraid of Stevie, but not as much as I used to be. He was afraid of my father.

Stevie wasn't the only one who avoided me. Most of the children in the camp were between the ages of eight and fourteen, but there were two girls my age, Doreen Connors and Jeannie Cain. They were always together and didn't want to have anything to do with me. I didn't want their company either. They enjoyed taunting me. When I walked past them, they would put their heads together and cup their hands over their mouths whispering and pointing in my direction. Sometimes they just snickered and turned away. Other times, they called me names like "ginger bap." Or they sang a stupid song, "Skinny ma link malojin legs, big banana feet." Then they laughed that cruel little laugh of girls who despised the very sight of their victim.

Jeannie lived with her mother, her grandmother and two scraggly, mangy-looking dogs. Her mother was called Dolly, and she looked like my idea of a true gypsy. She always wore a red and white flowered triangle scarf that she tied gypsy-style at the nape of her neck covering her black matted hair. Her dress was dirty, and grey ankle socks that were once white covered feet that were crammed into shoes a size too small. The heels of her scuffed black-laced shoes were so worn down on the outside that her legs bowed. I couldn't decide whether she had a swarthy complexion or her face was dirty. A large bump on the bridge of her thin, crooked nose completed the picture of a storybook gypsy.

Jeannie's grandmother looked like a witch and wore a permanent scowl on her mean, wizened face. Wisps of white hair sprung out from underneath a faded Black Watch tartan tam o' shanter. She was the oldest person I had ever seen and one of the scariest.

EIGHT

I had one friend, a quiet near-sighted boy called Freddie Corrigan. His mother was too poor to buy him glasses, so he squinted a lot and stood very close to anything he wanted to see. We had one thing in common; we both liked to draw. We had no pencils or paper, but at the edge of the camp stood one solitary wall, the only thing left of a building that had been bombed during the war. This wall was our blackboard and our easel. There was a pile of broken red bricks beside the wall, which Freddie and I discovered could be crushed to a red powder. A couple of unbroken bricks served as our pallets. We put the powder in the groove at the top of the brick and mixed the powder with spit to make a paste. We used a piece of brick with a sharp point to draw on the wall. We would spend hours drawing. I drew flowers and animals. Freddie was obsessed with drawing breasts and bums.

Sometimes we ran out of spit, but Freddie came up with the brilliant idea of peeing on the bricks. That way we could make a lot more red paste at once and spend more time drawing on the wall. One day, however, some strange notion came over Freddie. I was kneeling down, head bent low concentrating hard on crushing and mixing the pee and the red brick powder, when he turned his little white hose towards me and peed on my head. I jumped up and shouted with tears in my eyes and pee spilling over my face, blurring my vision.

"What did y' do that for, Freddie, I'm goin' ta tell your ma."

Freddie said nothing. He just buttoned up the fly in his trousers.

I stomped off in a rage with Freddie's pee dripping from my hair, running down my cheeks and onto my dress. By the time I reached Mrs. Corrigan's caravan, I was sobbing. In between sobs I explained to her what Freddie had done.

Mrs. Corrigan was a coarse, vulgar woman who cursed a lot. She was never seen without a cigarette, and she coughed so hard that I half expected her lungs to be spewed up into her hand along with the phlegmy brown spit. I heard her more often than I saw her, as she rarely came out of her caravan except for a few times around the campfire. She was unkempt in every way, and her hair looked like it had never been combed. It was usually hidden underneath a dark green scarf tied behind her head at the back of her neck. I began to care less about justice than about getting away from her, so I backed out of the caravan and ran back to ours.

I could hear her shouting in her hoarse voice, "Where's that dirty wee bugger? I'll give 'im a good hiden when I git 'im home."

Soon after, peeking from behind the army blanket, I saw Freddie's mother pulling him along by the ear heading for their caravan. She was still shouting.

"Jezez , Freddie, what the Christ did ya do that for? Did the divil himself take hol' d'ya? I'll skelp yer arse raw, ya dirty wee brute."

This was the second time I heard shouting and screaming from a caravan since my father and I joined the gypsies. I thought to myself that I'd probably lost Freddie as a friend.

There was very little water in the camp. Women would go with basins and pots to a little brook that ran down from the hills. Hauling water was hard work, so most of the water that was brought into the camp was used for cooking and not for washing.

The special circumstance involving Freddie prompted my father to make a special trip to the brook to get some water to wash my reeking hair. He used his shaving soap and scrubbed hard. I wondered whether I would have any hair or scalp left at the end of the ordeal. It got worse. The soap had to be rinsed out so I sat on the step of the caravan shivering, while my father poured cups of water over my head until all the soap was gone. Then he buried his nose in my hair and breathed deeply. "There yar nye, yer hair smells like daisies after a spring rain."

I thought the worst was over when he kissed my forehead and went into the caravan and got a couple of his hankies to dry my hair. He was rubbing my hair energetically when he stopped and drew in a long breath.

I looked at him. His eyes were wide with astonishment.

"Jezez, Kathleen, darlin', yer heads crawlin'. Yer ma'll kill me if I take ya back with yer head lousy like that."

He took a little black comb from his back pocket and started combing my hair. When he found what he was looking for, he put it on his thumbnail and squashed it with the other. When he located a nit he would slide it out by squeezing it between his thumb and index finger. It was a very slow, painful ordeal, and one that had to be repeated several times. I was sure I wouldn't have any hair left by the time he was done.

Peering closely at his two thumbs, he squished another one.

"Tryin' to keep those lousy wee buggers under control's goin' t'be a losin' battle 'cause I'm sure everybody in the camp's infested. M'self included," he added, scratching his head.

My hair was dry and I hoped lice-free. Even more important, my knickers were dry. It was suppertime, and I sat waiting on my bed in the caravan with clean, deloused hair and a fresh, dry pair of knickers. I probably hadn't noticed my head being itchy because the woollen knickers made my backside itch ten times worse.

My father went to Nora's to fetch our supper, and we ate as we did every night, in silence, sitting opposite each other on our beds. Supper was tripe, cooked in a broth made from sheep's elder and salt. Elder is fat scraped off the sheep's stomach and it was delicious. We ate the tripe with our hands then drank the broth.

We only had two meals a day, one early in the morning and one in the evening, so that when suppertime came we were too hungry to waste time talking.

After the meal, my father told me that there was to be a bit of a *ceilidh*. It was the thirty-first of October, All Saints' Eve. There would be another bonfire, and we would blacken our faces using soot from the fire. I thought a minute and counted backward. My thirteenth birthday had been two weeks ago, and it had come and gone without even a "Happy Birthday, Kathleen." I felt disappointed that my father hadn't remembered, but I decided to keep it to myself. Time wasn't important in the gypsy camp. I buried my disappointment in the same place I buried my loneliness and homesickness and asked my father why we had to blacken our faces.

"All Hallows Eve is the night that all the evil spirits are allowed to roam the earth. We blacken our faces so that they'll think we're one of them and they'll do us no harm."

My father carved a jack-o-lantern out of the damaged, stolen turnip. It was too bashed up to give to Nora, and it had been lying forgotten in a dark corner of the caravan for three days. It took him most of the day to carve it, working on it when he had free time. He bored a hole on each side and attached a string to make a handle. When it was finished, he put a candle in the middle and lit it. Suddenly, the face lit up. I was very pleased. I pressed my hands over my mouth to stop it from smiling any wider. I thanked my father and kissed his cheek and told him it was a wonderful jack-o-lantern. I held it up so that I could see what the face looked like with the candle shining through. It had a devilish grin on its pocked, scarred face. I thought of how jealous Doreen and Jeannie would be and smiled with satisfaction.

Music from the direction of the bonfire announced that the ceilidh had begun, and everyone emerged from their caravans.

A gypsy man called Desmond Delaney played the violin. I loved the sound of his sad, sweet music, but I didn't like to look at his disfigured face. The skin on the left side of his face was red and slid downward in smooth, shiny folds. My father told me he had been burned as a young man trying to save his family from a house fire, in which his wife and children perished. After losing his family and his face terribly disfigured, he felt he had nothing left to live for so he took refuge in the hills and lived like a hermit for a while until he eventually found a home with the gypsies. They don't seem to judge people by their appearance. It was obvious that Desmond was a trained musician; the music he played was so beautiful, I shivered with the sweetness of it.

My father played his mouth organ. Harry, a quiet, older man, played the concertina, which my father called a "malojin." Archie Mallon played the spoons, and a dirty-looking fellow everybody called Wild Billy banged on a big dented silver pot. Wild Billy's real name was William John Sheen. He wasn't as tall as my father, but he looked to weigh more. He liked to show off the tattoo of a hula dancer on his well-developed left bicep. With a twinkle in his eye, he would flex his bicep a certain way, and the hula dancer moved back and forth. Almost every day, Wild Billy could be seen throwing his knife at a bull's eye that he had drawn on a large wooden plank. Nora told me that Wild Billy spent most of his life running from the law and that it was best to stay clear of him. I was glad to comply. Billy could kill a rabbit on the run by throwing his knife and piercing its throat.

Police often came to the camp looking for Billy but gypsies had that "all for one and one for all" philosophy. When the officers asked for William Sheen, all the men in the camp claimed to be William Sheen. Gypsies had no identification papers so it was virtually impossible for the police to arrest any one man. Wild Billy always disappeared for three or four days after the police visit, and then he'd be sitting on the step of his caravan sharpening his knife on a stone as if nothing had happened.

NINE

Gypsies loved to dance, and on All Hallows Eve they danced around the fire with their faces blackened. The music and singing were grand. Men tapped their feet and clapped their hands while they watched the women dance around the fire with their skirts swirling like colourful spinning tops. It was a gloriously happy night. Even I forgot how lonely I was.

Wild Billy had stolen a couple of bottles of whiskey and before the night was over, everybody was drunk, including my father. At a little after midnight, people brought stools and chairs from their caravans and placed them around the dying fire. My father walked over to me and took my hand. He sat down on a stool, sat me on his knee and started singing:

"I'll take you home again, Kathleen,
across the ocean wild and wide.
To where your heart has ever been
since first you were my bonny bride.
The roses all have left your cheeks,
I've watched them fade away and die.
Your voice is sad when'er you speak
and tears bedim your loving eyes."

I put my head on his chest to be close and listened to him singing. The trouble with Irish songs is that they create a desperate longing inside you for what you miss the most. The words "I'll take you home" pierced my heart and a terrible feeling of emptiness washed over me. I wanted my mother. I needed her to hold me, to feel her warm sweet breath on my cheek as she held me. I wondered if I would ever see her again.

I sprang from my father's knee, kicking over the jack-o-lantern on the ground beside the chair. The candle spilled out and hissed and smoked in the damp grass. I pushed my way through a sea of laughing, blackened faces. In the caravan, I threw myself down on my little hard bed and cried. And then my father was pulling me into his arms.

"I'm so sorry, Cushla, darlin'. I thought that singin' that wee song with yer very name in it would make y' happy, but instead I've cut y' through to yer very soul. Shush, darlin', we'll be goin' home soon, I promise."

Through spasms of sobbing I wailed, "I hate this place, Daddy, and everyone in it. I want to go home where I belong. Nobody likes me here, the children do their best to torment me any way they can and my birthday was two weeks ago and you never remembered." Anger flared as I continued. "We were only supposed to stay here for a couple of days and we've been here six weeks."

I was inconsolable. Salty, warm tears streamed down my cheeks, wetting the front of my dress. My father cradled my head on his chest and stroked the back of my hair.

"Ach, Cushla, darlin', I'm sorry I forgot yer birthday. M' mind's ben on me trainin' for the boxin' and makin' money to get us home and I just forgot. Please forgive me. I'll make it up to you. We'll be goin' home soon. I promise."

I finally stopped crying, and he gently tucked me into bed.

"I love ya, darlin.' Go t'sleep now, and I'll be back in a wee while."

I felt so sad and homesick, and the walls of our sparse little caravan seemed to close in on me and make me feel worse than ever. I thought about what my mother and brothers were doing. Every Halloween my mother would make a "piggy puddin." She saved all the leftover stale bread for a week, and then she would soak it in buttermilk. Then she added currants, raisins, suet, allspice and cinnamon and put all it into a white pillowcase and boiled it for hours. This she put into a large tin pan and baked it. When it was done, she sliced it and poured custard over it, and we ate until we were stuffed. I buried my face in my pillow and sobbed.

When I finally stopped crying again, my attention was drawn to small, moving shadows on the ceiling. Rats were scurrying across the wooden ribs that supported the roof of the caravan. I was scared to death of them. I put my head under the blanket fearing that one of the rats might fall on my face. I remembered my mother's tale of a rat that climbed into a baby's pram and chewed its lips off.

I lay awake for a long time listening to the rats. They finally finished what they were doing and settled down or went out foraging for the night because the only sound was the crackling and spitting of the dying fire. I heard fewer and fewer voices until it was totally quiet in the camp. The celebration was over.

The curtain parted and my father stumbled in. I knew he was drunk—I could smell whiskey and he was clumsy as he moved about the caravan. He finally fell on his bed, clothes and all, and within seconds he was snoring loudly. I must have fallen asleep shortly after he came in because I don't remember anything after that until the usual clanging and splashing of the morning chamberpots.

It was Friday morning. All week, my father had been running around the camp shadow boxing and punching the side of the caravan. I had been dreading it, but my father was clearly excited at the thought of the boxing match. I followed him around like a puppy all day, and he sensed that I was worried about the fight. He wrapped some hankies around his fists and tied them in the palm of his hand and then he sat down beside me.

"Ach, Cushla, darlin', I'll be all right. I'll be back with a fistful o' five-pound notes. You be a good girl nye and go and find somebody to play with."

TEN

I had no intention of finding someone to play with, so I left my father to his training and set out for the field where the gypsies kept their horses. The sun was shining and it felt lovely and warm on my face. It had rained earlier, and the smell of the grass and the sweet sea air made me forget, for the moment, how unhappy I was. Halfway up the hill I stopped to pick some daisies and was about to settle down and make a daisy chain when Doreen and Jeannie appeared at the top of the hill.

Sensing danger, I grabbed my daisies and trotted back down the hill. They came after me, asking me why I had shoes when they did not. It wasn't fair, they chanted. I ran and they chased me. I lost my footing and tumbled to the bottom of the hill, leaving a trail of daisies behind me as I fell. I almost rolled right into the brook where the gypsies get their water. That's where the two mean-spirited girls found me, disoriented and a little bruised.

Doreen straddled me, pinning my arms above my head. Jeannie grabbed my kicking feet and wrenched my shoes off and dashed up the hill with them.

Sitting on my stomach, Doreen said, "Yer da's not here t' save ya this time. I've got ye just where I want ye."

At the top of the hill Jeannie shouted, "Come on, Doreen, this'll be a geg." Doreen finally got off me and sprinted after her.

I chased them, and being smaller and a lot thinner, I soon caught up. Jeannie, with my shoes in her hands, was running among the horses grazing in the field. She bent over and buried my white mutton dummies in a pile of horse dung, smearing it all over them and stuffing some inside. Doreen held me off until Jeannie hurled my dung-covered shoes back to me.

Doreen laughed nastily, "Yer wee shoes aren't so lovely nye, covered in horse shite, are they, ya uppity wee bitch."

In triumph, they walked passed me down the hill to the brook. Jeannie washed her hands, and then they strode towards the camp, their arms about each other's waists. I was furious enough to kill them both, but I just sank to my knees and cried over my ruined shoes. I was too defeated to think of revenge at the moment, but I'd get even eventually.

I picked up the defiled shoes by their laces and tried to avoid touching the clumps of dung. I held my foul-smelling shoes at arm's length, as far away from my nose as I could get them. I could still hear Doreen and Jeannie laughing as they headed back to camp.

I tried to wash my shoes in the brook, but they would never be as they were before. Now they were a pale mustard colour instead of the greyish white they'd become from wearing them night and day, rain or shine.

I was furious. I walked barefoot through the soft, thick grass back to the camp, thinking of ways to get my revenge. Doreen and Jeannie had separated and were going home to their caravans. I saw my opportunity at once. I would probably never be able to get back at both of them, so I would take double revenge on Jeannie.

I waited behind one of the caravans on the perimeter of the camp, and when Jeannie walked past, I dropped my sad white mutton dummies and sprang onto her back. My rage and thirst for revenge, and the smell from my own hands from carrying my dung scented shoes, doubled my strength.

Putting my left forearm around her neck and wrapping my legs around her ample waist, I pummelled her face with my right fist. She twisted and lurched forward, trying to shake me loose, but my two legs were planted firmly around her waist and my left arm was clamped around her neck like a vice. My right fist was wet and sticky from spattering blood over her face from her bleeding nose.

Tired with so much spinning and bucking, Jeannie's movements slowed and became clumsy and she collapsed to her knees. Still clinging to her back, her knees gave way and she fell flat on her belly. I grabbed her by the hair and repeatedly smashed her face into the dirt. I was thoroughly enjoying my revenge when I was pulled off her abruptly.

It was my father, and with a look of anger and disbelief on his face he said, "Kathleen McKenna, what in the name a God's got inta ya?"

Jeannie scrambled to her feet. Her face covered in a mixture of blood and dirt, she saw her opening and lunged at me, fists flying. My father grabbed her by the collar of her dress and was holding the two of us, flailing and kicking.

Jeannie's mother and granny heard the commotion and came running to see what all the noise was. Dolly snatched Jeannie from my father's grasp and inspected her face.

"What's happened t'ya, luv?"

Tears of pain and anger were streaming down Jeannie's face, making little white lines on her dirty, plump cheeks. Sniffling, she pointed in my direction. "That wee bitch over there did it. She jumped on m' back and smashed m' face into the dirt."

Jeannie's grandmother looked at my father and waggled a gnarled crooked finger at him.

"I wish ta God you'd go back ta where ya came from and take that wee guttersnipe with ya."

Old Mrs. Cain had long straggly white hair, a bump on her large crooked nose, several missing teeth, and she walked stooped over. Scolding my father, she had to tilt her head almost horizontally to look up into his face. Her voice sounded like a high-pitched yodel, and every joint on her thin gnarled fingers was swollen and bent, making them look like claws. She reminded me of the witch out of *Grimm's Fairie Tales*.

I tried to explain what Jeannie and Doreen had done, but it was no use. Everyone had painted me the villain since I was the one caught attacking Jeannie. Even so, my revenge was sweet and I felt content.

Back in our caravan, my father listened to my story about what had happened, and he only remarked, "Well, looks like I'm not the only McKenna to be boxin' the day."

He advised me that under the circumstances I should probably stay in the caravan for the rest of the day, and he didn't have to tell me not to wander around the camp that night when he went to town to fight. I wished I could go along with him, but children weren't allowed anywhere near a boxing ring.

He went over to Nora's and a few minutes later came back with our supper. He handed the smaller bowl to me and sat down on his own bed ready to enjoy his meal, when he turned his nose up and sniffed the air.

"Cushla, darlin', I think you should leave yer wee shoes outside the night. They're stinkin', and the fresh air might sweeten them up a wee bit." Pinching his nose between his thumb and index finger he took my foul-smelling shoes and tossed them out the door. "Tell y' the truth, luv, they're puttin me off m'supper."

He wiped his hands on the back of his trousers and sat back down to eat. We both ate greedily. There was no meat, just a bowl of boiled cabbage, but I was hungry with my exertions of the day and I thought it was delicious. I ate all the cabbage first and then drained the cabbage water to the last drop. After supper, my father took out his mouth organ and asked me if I wanted him to play me a wee tune before he left. I said no, because even happy songs made me feel too sad.

I put my arms around his neck and hugged him tightly. I told him I loved him and made him promise to knock the other man out quickly before he got hurt himself.

"That's just what I'm plannin' on doin', ma girl," he said confidently as he kissed my cheek and forehead.

"Goodnight, luv. Nye don't you be worryin'. Go t'sleep and I'll see ya in the mornin' and remember me in yer prayers."

I couldn't stand it. I felt as though I'd never see him again, and I didn't like the thought of being left in the camp alone. He turned to leave, I clutched his forearm and said, "Please, Daddy, can I walk to the edge of the field with ya?"

"All right, luv, but mind and wash the bowls and come straight back to the caravan."

Pulling aside the blanket, he jumped down from the caravan. I was about to step onto the rickety crate when he lifted me off, swinging me around several times before putting me down.

I managed a smile and took his warm, strong hand, and we set off.

By the time we reached the edge of the field, that worried, empty feeling in the pit of my stomach had returned. I hugged him tightly and kissed him goodbye and told him to come back safe. He practically had to pry my arms from around his neck.

I had made myself a necklace from a shell that I found on the seashore. The inside shimmered mauve and pink in the light. It was suspended around my neck by a piece of string stuck through a hole that I had made at the top of the shell. I took this, my only piece of jewellery, off and put it around his neck for good luck. And then I hugged and kissed him one last time. As he turned and started walking away, he said, "Run on back quickly now, Cushla, yer gittin' cold."

I watched him until he disappeared over the hill.

I ran back to the caravan to get the bowls. I took them over the hill to the brook and washed them and dried them on my skirt.

The water was icy cold and I shivered, so I ran back to the caravan, lit the candle and got into bed and listened to the camp noises outside. Sometimes I could make out bits of conversation, which was mostly about a daring theft and how they nearly got caught.

ELEVEN

I was just about to blow out the candle and go to sleep when the grey army blanket parted and Wild Billy's face appeared. He came in and sat down on my father's bed. He smelled really bad.

Annoyed at his intrusion, I asked sharply, "What d'ya think yer doin'? Git outta here this minute or I'll yell fer Nora."

Ignoring my outburst, he sniffled and wiped his nose on his sleeve. "Ach, since yer da's gone inta town and left ya, I thought I'd come and keep y'company fer a wee while."

Holding the blanket under my chin, I told him I didn't need any company. I was just fine on my own. Trying to sound braver than I felt, I said, "Sure m'da's gone t'fight in a boxin' match and he's goin' t'win, and if I tell him that you came into our caravan when he wasn't here you'll be very sorry indeed."

He snickered and leaned over to wrap his coarse, rough fingers around my wrist. He pulled me out of bed and onto his knee. I resisted, but I was no match for the strength of a grown man. Rigid muscular arms held me firmly, and I could smell whiskey off his breath. "If I were you, ma girl," he leered, "I wouldn't mention this wee visit to yer da or you might be the one to be very sorry. Besides, yer Uncle Billy's just come t'say good night and tuck y'in."

I was wearing only my yellow woollen nickers and my thin, worn cardigan, and I was both cold and scared. I felt self-conscious and sat shivering on his knee. I told him that Nora was coming over to say good night and tuck me in any minute. He didn't pay me any mind and slid one hand down the soft inside of my right thigh while he rubbed my back with the other. "I'll be leavin' in a wee while, and as far as Nora's concerned, her house's in darkness and I expect she's in 'er bed fer the night."

I could hardly breathe for fear of him. My heart was pounding loud and fast. I didn't want to look into those evil eyes, so I focused on my tightly clasped hands on my lap.

The tone of his voice changed to a breathless whisper. "Give me yer hand a wee minute."

He pried my hands apart and guided my right hand in between his legs. He was breathing shallow noisy breaths that smelled of whiskey. I tried to pull away. He hurt my hand with clenching it so tight and forcing it down against the hard bulge in his crotch.

Wild Billy was concentrating on what was happening between his legs, and I saw my opportunity. With all the strength I could muster, I wrenched my hand from his grip. I sprung free. I ran for the door, but Wild Billy thrust out his hand, grazing my leg. I stumbled, but regained my balance, and was just about to escape through the army blanket when Wild Billy's steely fingers dug into my shoulder. He crushed me back against him. One arm around my neck made it hard to breathe, while his other hand pulled my knickers down. He forced his probing fingers between my legs and rubbed his bulging groin hard against my bottom. I had been too frightened to make a noise, but now I managed a single faint scream before he took his hand from between my legs and clamped it over my mouth.

"Ya don't want t'be doin' that nye, do ya," he hissed. "We're just havin' a wee bit a fun. Aren't we?"

Just then the army blanket was flung open, and Nora burst in with a hammer raised over her head, anger burning in those piercing brown eyes. She was growling like an animal.

"Take your filthy hands off that wee girl! Git outta here and niver set foot in this caravan or bother this wee girl again or I'll tell 'er da and he'll skin ye alive. De ya hear me!"

Wild Billy was more surprised at being caught than anything.

"Ach, sure, I wasn't goin' ta hurt her."

Nora narrowed her eyes and made scary noises in her throat. "Just git outta my sight."

Wild Billy released me, and I fell to the hard wooden floor of the caravan coughing and gasping. My throat felt raw. Nora helped me up and put her arms around me. "Are ye all right, luv? He'll not be botherin' ye again, I'll see ta that."

In a moment, she said, "Would y' like a cup o' tea, luv, or a wee hot whiskey to calm yer nerves?"

I shuddered. "No thanks, Nora, I just want t'get into bed. I need t'lie down."

She hugged me and said, "Well then, just you git inta yer bed and think no more about that dirty oul brute. I'll give 'im a good talkin' to. Go t'sleep, luv, and I'll see ya in the mornin'."

After she left, it took me a long time to get to sleep. I didn't feel safe without my father, especially after what had just happened. Although I didn't feel cold, my teeth chattered, and I lay in bed shivering. I kept thinking of Doreen holding me down and Jeannie stuffing my shoes with horse dung. I kept repeating over and over in my mind what had just happened with Wild Billy. The only good thing that had happened today was getting back at Jeannie, smashing her face into the dirt.

The stink of Wild Billy lingered on my skin and up my nose, and I could still feel his fingers moving between my legs. I wished for some water to wash the feel of him off me.

I said my prayers and, as though God knew I needed something to calm me down after such a horrible day, it started to rain. The sound of the rain hitting the wooden roof of the caravan was almost the only thing I truly loved about my gypsy life. It soothed me and finally lulled me to sleep.

The next morning, I looked over and there was my father safe in his bed. I slung myself around the bed and bent over towards him to get a closer look. He had a cut over his left eye, making his eyebrow look like it was in two parts. His eyelid was blue and puffy, and there was blood crusted in his nostrils. Clutched in his left hand was the little shell I had put around his neck, the string broken. I took it from his hand and retied the string and put it back around my neck. By the look of his bruised, battered face, it hadn't brought him any luck. He opened his good eye and smiled at me.

"Top o' the mornin' to ya, darlin'," he said cheerfully as if he hadn't a care in the world.

He reached for his trousers, groped in the pockets, and pulled out a handful of silver shillings and a roll of pound notes. He was glowing with pride.

"Yer old da's made fifteen quid in one night. Can ye believe it, Cushla, darlin'? We'll be on our way home in no time."

I tried to share his enthusiasm. I hugged him, tears streaming down my cheeks in spite of myself.

"There now, what's the matter? Are ye worried about the state of m'face? Don't be botherin' yer head about that. In a couple a days, I'll be good as new and ready to fight again and make another fifteen quid or more." Fifteen pounds was a lot of money because I remember my mother paying the rentman two shillings a week for our house in Belfast.

I was concerned about the state of his face, but I was thinking about what happened with Wild Billy the night before. I decided not to tell my father; he would be worried and angry, and he would probably give Billy a good beating. He didn't need any more of that at the moment, and I didn't think that Billy would come to the caravan again. He was afraid of Nora and Archie, and I was positive he didn't want any trouble from my father, either. Besides, if he were thrown out of the camp, he would have nowhere to live.

After getting dressed, my father and I paid our usual morning visit to Nora and Archie's house for breakfast. He didn't usually come in with me, but that morning he did. Nora was waiting for me at the table with a steaming bowl of salty porridge, and Archie was still lying, snoring on his dirty, stained mattress in the corner.

With a battered smile, he presented Nora with a five-pound note.

She stared at him. "Well, ya cud niver tell by lookin' at yer face, but ye musta won last night."

"Aye, I did."

She made the sign of the cross. "God bless ya, Jimmy, and may the saints preserve ya." Brows furrowed knowingly she said to me. "What about you, luv, are y'all right this mornin'?" I told her I was doin' all right. She came and put her arm around my shoulder and said, "That's good, luv, nye eat yer breakfast 'fore it gits cold."

On our way back to the caravan, my father said to me, "Do you and Nora have a wee secret between yez that y'don't want yer oul da to know about?" Sheepishly I lied.

"No, Daddy, we don't."

Raising his split right eyebrow, a sign that he wasn't totally convinced I was telling the truth, he put his arm around me and pulled me to him and said, "All right, luv, but I'll be keepin' me eye on you two."

He regained his high spirits as he recounted each uppercut and jab with as much detail and gusto as if boxing were a painless sport, sort of like dancing. I got a blow by blow description of how he won the fight.

TWELVE

One sunny day after we had been with the gypsies for two months, I was lying on my belly in the soft grass beside the brook. I was concentrating on an ant dragging a dead fly twice its size up over some rocks, when movement on the other side of the water caught my eye.

Curious, I jumped across the brook to investigate. It was a grey army blanket undulating beneath a large willow tree. More puzzled still, I stepped closer to investigate. Something or someone was rolling around underneath it. I lifted up a corner of the blanket.

I was completely shocked and embarrassed at what I had discovered, and I was not the only one. Glaring up at me with a look of utter disbelief was a totally naked Tom Sullivan on top of a spread-eagled and equally naked Ginny Sloan. Most of her was hidden but you couldn't mistake Ginny for anybody else. She had the brightest red-gold hair and when the sun abruptly flashed on her naked body, the fuzzy mound between her thighs glowed a bright fiery orange. Light brown freckles dusted her flailing pale-skinned legs.

A startled look on her face soon turned to anger. Her cheeks were pink as she struggled to push Tom off.

I dropped the blanket and ran.

"Hey you, Kathleen McKenna, come back here a wee minute. I want t'talk to ya!"

Still running, I glanced back and saw Tom Sullivan sprinting after me, pulling up his trousers as he ran. The sight was comical, and only my keen sense of immediate danger kept me from laughing. I had just seen him in all his naked glory. His skin tanned from working in the fields with the horses and his stomach muscles hard and strong. He caught up to me and spun me around.

"Now listen, you sleekit wee bitch, if you tell a soul about what you've seen, yer life'll not be worth livin'. So keep yer mouth shut. D'ya hear me?"

Scared, but also suppressing a giggle, I promised I wouldn't say a word to anyone.

That promise wouldn't be hard for me to keep because I hardly spoke to anyone other than Nora and my father.

Nora had told me that Tom Sullivan had been orphaned at the age of twelve. His father had strangled his mother to death in a fit of rage; then Tom's Uncle Leonard, his mother's brother, killed Tom's father and went to jail for life. Tom had no other family, so he lived on the streets for a year or so, eventually landing in the Borstal School for Delinquent Boys for habitual stealing. Some of the boys were hardened criminals and were put there to protect society. Tom hated the Borstal and ran away after six months. He joined the gypsies when he was fourteen and had been with them ever since. He told my father that he thought he was about twenty. He never went to school other than the Borstal, where he had learned to sign his name. He could neither read nor write, but he could count, add and subtract. Tom had a special way with horses and spent most of his day with them. The gypsies depend on horses for transportation, so Tom's contribution to the gypsy camp was important.

Tom liked my father. He listened to my father's boxing stories and offered himself as a sparring partner. I hoped that he wouldn't get too interested in boxing because, while my father was a handsome man, every feature on Tom's face was perfect. He had ice-blue eyes that never looked mean, framed by black eyebrows and long thick eyelashes. His white, even teeth seemed marvellous in the gypsy camp where everyone else's teeth were brown or gone. He was tall and slender, but with well-defined muscles. He wore a little gold hoop in his right earlobe.

I was only thirteen, but sometimes when I saw him riding a horse with the wind blowing his black curly hair, my heart pounded of its own accord. I slipped into daydreams of sitting behind him with my arms around him holding him close and my cheek pressed against his back. This dream somehow didn't square with what I had seen under the blanket.

That night sitting in the candlelit caravan, I wanted to tell my father what I had seen, but I didn't. Instead, I listened to his stories about when he went to London and got a job in a hotel. He would describe the food and the wonderful desserts and what rich ladies were wearing and how much gold and jewellery they had on.

Rudyard Kipling was his favourite poet. He had memorized quite a few of his poems and would recite them to me. I loved the way he emphasized, "you're a better man than I am, Gunga Din." The memory of my father's soft Irish brogue reciting those poems stayed with me forever.

THIRTEEN

One morning soon after the day I discovered Tom and Ginny under the blanket, I found my father sitting on the crate outside our caravan, wrapped in the army blanket from his bed. He had just struck a match to light a thin, crooked cigarette. I walked over to him, rubbing the sleep from my eyes.

"Good mornin', Daddy. You're up early."

The swelling in his right eye had gone down, so he was able to look up at me with both eyes.

"Good mornin', luv."

He lit his cigarette, inhaled, and flipped the match onto the damp ground where it sputtered and smoked.

"Well, ma girl, I've somethin' t'tell ye. There's ben a death in the camp."

The lack of emotion in his voice told me it wasn't someone either of us would miss, and I was right. It was old Mrs. Cain. She had died in her sleep, and Dolly and some of the women were preparing her for the wake and burial.

The camp was more alive today than ever. It seemed strange to me that a death could bring the camp to an unaccustomed state of liveliness and energy. The women were bustling in and out of Mrs. Cain's caravan. Dolly was seen from time to time, her eyes red-rimmed from crying, and she had that lost, "what-am-I-going-to-do-without-you" look.

Mrs. Cain was to be buried in the morning, and the wake would begin at suppertime.

Nora sent Tom Sullivan and Ginny Sloan to town to buy flour, sugar, salt and a small amount of white pepper with some of the money my father had given her. Salt and pepper were precious commodities, as they were the only seasonings used for flavouring food.

While the women were preparing old Mrs. Cain for burial, some men went into town to nick some whiskey. My father and three other men went into the hills at the back of the camp to steal a sheep. They would skin it and gut it in the field, bring the carcass back to camp and hang it in Nora and Archie's back scullery.

Children were sent into the fields to gather wildflowers and willow branches to be placed around Mrs. Cain's deathbed. Old Mrs. Cain had been with the gypsies for a long time and they wanted to give her a proper send-off.

After the funeral supper of meaty mutton stew, my father took me by the shoulders.

"Now darlin', I want ya ta go in and pay yer respects to old Mrs Cain. I know ya didn't like her much, and she felt the same about you, but it'll be expected of ya just the same."

I put off going to pay my respects to old Mrs. Cain as long as I could, until the sun had nearly disappeared behind the trees. I had to go now or it would be dark. I was the last one to go, and I had to go alone. Everyone was standing in front of Mrs. Cain's caravan talking and drinking. I walked to the caravan slowly, keeping my head down, being careful not to make eye contact with anyone. I stood outside the door, dreading going in. I hadn't liked the look of her alive, so I was sure I wouldn't like the look of her dead.

I tiptoed up the creaky wooden steps so as not to disturb her. Before entering, I hesitated and took a deep breath. I drew the curtain back slowly and stood in the threshold until my eyes got used to the dim candlelit room. Her thin form was barely noticeable stretched out on the bed.

At first, I thought that she had two holes where her eyes were supposed to be, but as I drew nearer and my eyes adjusted to the darkness, I saw that they were pennies, placed there to keep her eyes shut. Her hands were clasped on top of the sheet that covered her, and black and silver rosary beads were wrapped around her gnarled fingers. Her ghostly silver-white hair was spread out like two wings at each side of her head. Two bricks on her chest were just visible under the sheet, holding her down on the bed. Mrs. Cain's back was so crooked that the women who were preparing her body for burial had a difficult time keeping her flat without the weight of the bricks.

Wildflowers and willow branches hanging from the ceiling made the dimly lit caravan smell almost pleasant, but the candles cast eerie flickering shadows on the wall. I panicked and bolted for the door. In my hurry to get out, I kicked the leg of the bed and the jolt dislodged the bricks from her chest. She sprang upright. The pennies flew off and landed on the sheet. Her colourless eyes were wide open staring at me and a loud belch issued from her gaping mouth. She was a growling spectre from hell.

I screamed and threw myself out the door, falling headfirst down the stairs and scraping my shins on the rough steps. Everyone ran to the caravan and the women hurried inside. I heard one of them say, "Mother of God, that's a sign."

My father helped me up and looked at my bleeding shins. "What in the name o' God's happened ta ya now?"

I was crying hysterically and shaking so hard I could scarcely speak. I tried to tell him that Old Mrs. Cain had sat right up in her bed and looked straight at me and growled. I said, in between sobs, "She hated me for hittin' Jeannie so she came back to haunt me."

Putting his arms around me, my father sighed, and the impatience vanished from his face and voice. "Now listen to me, darlin', she can't do that, she's dead and gone. Go back to the caravan, luv, and wait for me there. I'll go and find out what's happenin'."

I sat on the step of the caravan for a long time crying and rocking back and forth, not wanting to go inside. I heard loud, excited voices. I couldn't make out what they were saying, but much of the altercation involved my father and Dolly Cain. He finally came over and sat down beside me and told me what had really happened. I had kicked the bed and knocked the bricks off Mrs. Cain's chest. With nothing to hold her down, she sat up and the pennies fell off her eyes.

I wanted to believe this version, but mostly, I still believed she had come back to frighten the life out of me for hitting Jeannie. Everyone else in the gypsy camp believed that, too. They said it was a sign that Mrs. Cain did not want me at her funeral. That was fine with me; I didn't want to go.

The rest of the evening was uneventful. Before dark I climbed into my damp, cold bed, shivering not only from the cold, but also from the image of the old Mrs. Cain springing up at me like a banshee from hell.

Later, my father came in drunk and passed out on his bed. When he began to snore, I finally relaxed and fell asleep until a loud knock and Tom Sullivan's voice woke us both. "Right, Jimmy, it's time t'get up."

My father got up and left, but I, not being welcome at the funeral, looked through a narrow crack in the wall of our caravan.

The sun was barely over the horizon. Everyone in the camp was standing outside Dolly Cain's caravan beside a long flat cart. Sam Corrigan, Freddy's father, hitched a large black horse to the cart. A black ostrich feather fluttered between the horse's ears, and a purple and gold cloth covered its back.

Four men came out of Dolly Cain's caravan carrying something that looked like an Egyptian mummy from the Belfast Museum. It was old Mrs. Cain wrapped tightly with ropes in a white sheet. They laid her body on the cart, and Dolly and Jeannie climbed in beside it. Sam Corrigan took hold of the bridle and started walking toward the back field. The mourners followed in solemn procession. My father and Tom Sullivan came last, carrying spades.

I was happy to skip the funeral, but I wanted to know what they would do with old Mrs. Cain's body. Seeing her buried deep in the ground would make me feel safer. I waited until they had a good head start, and then I followed.

They walked over the wet, grassy fields for half an hour and stopped at the bottom of a remote hill away from the camp and even farther away from farmer Donnelly's farmhouse.

I lay on my belly on a small hill close enough to watch, but far enough away to stay hidden.

My father and Tom dug the grave quickly. The sun was just burning through the heavy morning mist as old Mrs. Cain's body was lowered into the grave. The terrible sound of women wailing echoed through the rising mist. I had never liked the old woman, but the mournful wailing and weeping made me sad. I shed a tear at the thought of Dolly having to live her whole life without her mother.

Mrs. Cain had been a Catholic, so Nora read from the Bible. When she stopped, she sprinkled a handful of earth over Mrs. Cain's body and turned away from the grave. With her head bowed, holding the Bible to her chest, she walked over to Dolly and Jeannie. She hugged them both and they wailed even louder. Then everyone headed back to camp.

My father and Tom Sullivan stayed behind to fill in the grave and replace the grass over it. When they were finished no one would know that there was a grave there. There was no marker, so no one ever would.

I ran back to camp and got back into bed so no one would know that I had watched the funeral. When my father came in, he sat down on his bed and rested his elbows on his knees.

"Well, Cushla, darlin', are ya awake? That was a sight to be seen. No coffin! Not even a wooden box, she was just wrapped in a sheet and put in the ground. I've niver seen the like of it. Anyway, she's laid to rest in their fashion."

I confessed to my father that I had followed the funeral procession and watched everything from the top of the hill. He laughed.

"Yer a sleekit wee imp! You're turnin' out to be a holy terror. I don't know what I'm goin' ta do with ya. Let's just keep that wee bit o' information to ourselves."

My father moved over to my bed and put his sweaty arm around me. "There's to be a wake the night for old Mrs. Cain," he said hugging me close to him. "I'll be busy the day gittin' wood for the bonfire, so please try to stay clear a trouble. D'ye think ye can do that fer yer da?"

I said I would try. He winked at me, kissed my cheek and left.

I felt awkward asking the women of the camp if I could help, so I asked Nora if there was anything I could do for her. She was busy making soda bread with the flour and salt that Tom and Ginny had brought back from town. It must have been a change for them actually having money to pay for it. Nora told me that I could keep the fire going under the bricks so that the griddle she was making the bread on would stay hot. When we finished, eight cakes of soda bread lay side by side.

Everything was finally ready for the wake. The bonfire stacked with wood took on a life of its own after being lit. The sheep had been cut in two and roasted on spits over two fires outside Nora and Archie's house. A large kettle of potatoes and cabbage bubbled noisily in the kitchen. Everyone stood around the roaring bonfire talking to one another with tin cups and plates in their hands, waiting for Nora to call everyone to supper.

Nora asked Tom Sullivan to bring the big black cauldron filled with the potatoes and cabbage out and put it on the ground. Then she called to me.

"Kathleen, luv, wud ye go in an git the big basket with the soda bread and put it on that chair b' the door?"

That was her way of telling everyone I was welcome at the wake, and Nora always got the last word.

The two halves of the sheep were done, one of them slightly charred, so Archie doused the fires under them and sharpened his knife on a stone. Wild Billy appeared from behind his caravan carrying a large jug over each shoulder. He walked to where Archie was sitting.

"I managed to nick a couple a jugs a poteen from old Donnelly's woodshed, so drink up, Archie, we're sure ta have a good night."

Archie patted Wild Billy on the back. "Aye, indeed we will."

He removed the cork and slung the jug up 'till it rested on his shoulder and then tilted his head back and poured poteen into his mouth. He coughed and spluttered and handed it to Wild Billy, who did the same. He smacked his lips and wiped them on the sleeve of his coat and replaced the cork. Everyone gathered around the two men and held their cups out to be filled. I thought to myself that it's a wonder old farmer Donnelly had anything left after being robbed of sheep from his fields, vegetables from his garden, and now poteen from his woodshed.

Nora called everyone to come to supper, and the wake began. With a large ladle, she portioned out the potatoes and cabbage, and Archie cut generous slices of mutton.

After we had all eaten our fill, chairs and stumps of trees were placed around the bonfire and musical instruments were fetched. From the middle of the circle, Nora called for everyone's attention.

"We're all here the night to bid farewell to one of our dearest friends just departed this life, Josie Cain. We'll all miss her and we'll do our best for her daughter, Dolly, and her granddaughter, Jeannie. So lift yer glass and drink to Josie Cain. God take care o' ye, Josie." Nora shot the whiskey back in one gulp.

Everyone shouted, "To Josie, God bless ye!"

Sam Corrigan added, "An' may ye be a half hour in heaven b'fore the divil knows yer dead." That got him a poke in the ribs from his wife.

My father started playing "The Wild Colonial Boy" on his mouth organ, and Desmond Delaney joined him playing his violin. It was a beautiful song, and the haunting melody so sweet it brought tears to my eyes. Everyone sang and the jug of whiskey was passed around. As more whiskey was drunk and the music got livelier, some of the women got up to dance.

My father took a long swig of whiskey and started playing "I'll Tell Me Ma When I Get Home." It was a lively tune and everyone knew the words, and pretty soon everybody was singing and clapping their hands. Even I felt myself caught up in the merriment of the moment.

Ginny Sloan loved to be the centre of attention. Her red-gold hair was flying as she danced around the fire, flouncing her yellow and blue skirt like a moth taunting the flames. She pranced up to my father and swirled her skirt upward over his head and then spun around, giving him and everyone else a glimpse of her bare backside. He stopped playing to catch his breath, affected, no doubt, by the sight of Ginny's exposed, naked bottom. Realizing her effect on him, she danced behind him and put her arms around his neck, resting her breasts on his shoulders. He took another long drink from the whiskey jug and winked at me.

"I guess I've still got it with the girls."

Tom Sullivan pulled Ginny away from my father and kissed her hard on the mouth. Ginny pushed him away.

Fire blazing in her amber eyes, she snapped, "Catch yerself on, Tom Sullivan, you don't own me."

He went to grab for her again, but she stopped him by a loud stinging smack to his face. Everyone laughed and cheered as she flounced her skirt and danced away. Tom Sullivan rubbed his cheek. He took solace in the jug of poteen that was being passed around and took a long swig.

Ginny Sloan was as pretty as her mother Annie was ugly. She was slim, but curvaceous, and she had the self-confidence that only really good-looking people possess. Red-gold hair framed her beautiful face. She had flawless alabaster skin with a faint dusting of freckles. But her smoldering amber eyes were her most striking feature. Her full lips were parted in a wide smile as she danced among the gypsies without a shred of inhibition.

My father was getting drunk, but he was happy, so I was glad. The music was fast and lively, and everyone was drunk and dancing. Doreen and Jeannie stopped every so often to stick their tongues out at me and turn their backs to me and fling their skirts up exposing their backsides to me.

Nora told me to loosen up a wee bit and dance. I tried my best, but I felt awkward and quietly resumed my seat away from the fire and the dancers. I sat for a while, and when I began to get tired and bored, I walked over to my father and told him I was going to go to bed. He stopped playing and whacked the mouth organ several times on the palm of his hand to get rid of spittle.

"Right ye are, luv," he said, slurring his words. " I'll see ye in the mornin'."

I kissed him on the cheek and left. I could hear laughter and singing well into the night, and eventually fell asleep.

I was awakened some time later by a scuffling sound outside the caravan. I listened for a few minutes trying to identify the noise. There was heavy breathing and soft moaning coming from the doorstep. I slid out of bed and tiptoed over to the army blanket and pulled it aside.

I was appalled at what I saw. My father was holding Ginny Sloan's bare breast, while he kissed it passionately. Her head was thrown back and her flame-coloured hair shimmered like burnished gold in the moonlight. The two of them were so enraptured, they didn't realize I was standing right behind them confused and dumbfounded.

"Daddy," I cried out. "What are you doin'?"

With the shock of hearing my voice, my father staggered backward knocking over the crate in front of the caravan.

When I looked up, Ginny had vanished into the night. My father noisily replaced the rickety crate and stumbled into the caravan.

Swaying back and forth, he said thickly, "I'm awful sorry, darlin', I lost m'head for a minute. Thanks for comin' out and savin' me from doin' somethin' I would've regretted."

He staggered to his bed and collapsed and fell asleep with his legs dangling over the side. I pulled off his boots and lifted his legs up on the bed. I stood looking down at his bruised, handsome face, thinking how much I hated Ginny Sloan. This never would've happened if she hadn't been whirling around him all night showing off her bare backside.

By the time I woke up the next morning, my father was already running around the outside perimeter of the camp, stopping every so often to spar with Tom Sullivan, who was running along beside him. I sat down on the grass and watched him. Last night seemed like a long time ago, and the incident with Ginny Sloan was almost forgotten.

After he finished his training, my father sat down on the grass beside me.

"Cushla, darlin', I'm sorry about last night. I can hardly recall what happened, but I know I must've disappointed ye. I love yer ma, and that'll niver happen again." He put his arm around my shoulder and gave me a breathless, sweaty hug.

"I've got somethin' important I want to talk to you about," he said.

I put my head on his shoulder. "What is it, Daddy?"

He reached into his back pocket and took out a little tin box and a thin, blue-coloured packet of cigarette papers with a picture of a bearded sailor in the corner. After rolling the tobacco up in the paper, he licked the glue-covered edge and ran his finger down the middle to seal it. He stuck it in his mouth and lit it and took a long drag, blowing the smoke away from me and spitting a couple of times to dislodge loose bits of tobacco from his tongue.

Using his fingers to pick out the last piece he said, "Well, Kathleen, darlin', we've ben here now for over two months. Since there's no chance of you gittin' a job in this wee town, I suggest y'go back to school while yer here. There's a wee school just down the road from here on the way ta town, and I think it would be a good idea for you t'go."

"But, Daddy, I thought we weren't goin' to be here much longer."

"Well, luv, I'm hopin' we'll be home for Christmas, but that's still a month away, and you're missin' a lot of school."

I was almost in tears. "I thought we'd be leavin' in a couple of days since you got all that money."

He winked at me. "Aye, but I'll be makin' a whole lot more than that, darlin'. I plan to go home to yer ma with enough money to get us to Canada or America."

I didn't want to leave Ireland to go to America, or anywhere else for that matter, so I sat looking down at my feet and said nothing.

My father hugged me. "Niver you worry, everything'll turn out all right. Even if you're only there for a month, it'll do y'good and help pass the time. Now this afternoon, we'll take a wee walk to that school and see about gittin' you enrolled."

FOURTEEN

One of the few tolerable aspects of life with the gypsies was not going to school. But my father was determined that I should go, and I had no choice in the matter, so I combed and plaited my hair and tied the ends with the blue ribbon that my mother had tied my hair with before I left home. I took my navy dress out of the suitcase. It was wrinkled from being crushed, so I spread it out on my bed and tried to smooth the stubborn creases. I gave up on the wrinkles and put it on anyway. Why did I have to go when the other gypsy children didn't?

"These childer know no other kind o' life. Yer ma and me know better. T'git on in life, y'need an education, and we want what's best fer you and yer brothers."

Then he grabbed my hand and pulled me along because the conversation was finished.

We set off down the narrow, winding road towards the old grey stone schoolhouse on the outskirts of Ballymacruise. Over the door I noticed a name and date carved on the cement inlay and read it aloud, "Flynn Memorial, 1908."

We went in. The old school had the same terrible musty smell that our old neighbourhood library in Belfast did. Everything seemed grey, including the tall, severe woman who came forward to greet us—her clothes, her hair, her glasses. Even her face looked grey. Without moving her head, she looked down her nose at me through the bottom of her glasses and then back up to my father.

She spoke as if the collar of her blouse was buttoned too tightly around her throat, strangling her.

"Yes, what is it you want?" Her enunciation was flawless.

My father wasn't a bit put off by her haughty manner and replied confidently, "Yes, good morning to y', ma'am. I'm James McKenna and this is m'daughter Kathleen. I'm here to enroll 'er in yer school."

Stiffly she said, "You're the boxer, I believe, and you and your daughter are living with the gypsies. Is that correct, Mr. McKenna?"

"At the moment, yes, ma'am, that is correct, but I don't see what that has to do with m'daughter attendin' yer school."

"Well, you see, Mr. McKenna, we don't enroll gypsies in our school."

From the look on my father's face, I could tell his patience was wearing thin. He took a long deep breath and exhaled slowly.

"We're not gypsies," he said evenly. "I have identification papers for both m'self and m'daughter, and she has every right to attend yer school." He held out the papers.

She looked down at them for a moment before taking them from his hand. After taking several minutes to scrutinize them thoroughly, she handed the papers back to my father.

"Everything appears to be in order. Come with me, please."

She led us into an office and told us to take a seat. Walking to her desk without turning around, she said, "My name is Miss Glover, and I am the school secretary."

She asked my father a lot of questions, including our address.

"As you well know, Miss Glover, we do not actually have an address at the moment. Y'could put Killaughy Road and leave it at that."

Miss Glover removed her glasses, clasped her hands on the desk in front of her and said in mock astonishment. "Mr. McKenna, how do you expect me to believe that you are not gypsies when you have no fixed address?"

My father told her very slowly that we had a fixed address in Belfast, but were living with the gypsies until he found a job.

Then, with conviction, he said, "Every child in this country has the right t'go to school, and my daughter is no exception. If y'don't let her attend, I'll write to the School Board and see what they have to say."

Taken off guard by my father's determination, she backed off.

My father answered the rest of the questions and after he signed the form, Miss Glover said I could start attending right away. I couldn't believe that any of this was real. I didn't want to go to school, especially her school, now or ever.

Miss Glover got up and went to a cupboard and took out a slate, some chalk, a jotter and a pencil. She handed them to me and told my father that he could leave now as she had all the necessary information.

"Good day, Mr. McKenna," she said, dismissing him abruptly. "School is finished at four o'clock."

I felt dejected. I lowered my head and fixed my eyes on my shoes. My father turned to me and took me by the shoulders.

"Now, Cushla, darlin', you be a good girl and learn yer lessons. I'll be back for ya at four o'clock. Goodbye, luv."

I whispered, "Goodbye, Daddy," and he strode out of the room.

I was alone with Miss Glover. I didn't like her, and from her attitude and the expression of superiority on her face, I knew she didn't like me. She glowered at me. School didn't look promising.

"You'd better behave yourself, young lady. We tolerate no nonsense in this school. Now follow me. Your master's name is Mr. Spencer. He's one of our best teachers."

She said nothing as she led me down a long corridor. The only two sounds were the clacking of her shoes on the hardwood floor and my heart, beating loudly and thumping twice as fast as her footsteps. I was sure everyone behind those closed doors could hear it as well.

At the bottom of the corridor, she opened a door and propelled me through it. Mr. Spencer was standing by the blackboard holding a piece of chalk.

Miss Glover raised her right eyebrow, sucked in her cheeks and said with exaggerated deference, "Mr. Spencer, this is Kathleen McKenna from the gypsy camp. She will be joining your class. I have explained what is expected of her, and so I leave her in your capable hands."

Mr. Spencer was a tall man with rounded shoulders. His neck was long and thin, and his Adam's apple featured prominently, bobbing up and down when he spoke. His nostrils twitched, but he didn't say anything. Finally, he pointed to a seat at the back of the second row.

"Sit down there and be quick about it. You've held up the class long enough."

The children snickered and giggled as I passed down the row. Mr. Spencer whacked his bamboo cane on his desk and shouted, "QUIET!" I jumped and my heart raced faster than ever. I thought to myself, I hate this place. I want to go home. It didn't take long to recognize that Mr. Spencer was not a kind or patient teacher. He was cold and unfriendly.

Mr. Spencer called attendance, which was acknowledged quickly by each student replying "present."

The day, nevertheless, had its lighter moments. A funny thing happened that first afternoon that made me giggle. Mr. Spencer passed out new lesson books and told us to put our names on the front. He walked down each row to see that we had all done it properly. But when he came to a slovenly, sleepy-looking boy, he stopped and said, "You've left the 'y' off the end of your name," he drawled sarcastically. "Correct it immediately."

The boy did as he was told. Mr. Spencer became agitated and told the boy to stand up and tell every one his name. The boy stood up slowly.

"M'name's Gregory McIver."

Mr. Spencer picked up his book and said, "Well, you ejit, it says here this book belongs to Gregor McIvery."

The class laughed, which caused Mr. Spencer to whack his bamboo cane on Gregory's desk.

Finally it was four o'clock. My father was outside waiting for me. I ran to him and grabbed his hand. I was very glad to be going back to the gypsy camp, which felt more like home than it ever had before. My father asked me how I liked school, and I told him I didn't. But I told him about Gregory McIvor, and he laughed.

When we got to the caravan it was nearly time for supper, so I took off my navy blue dress and put on my everyday one. We went to Nora's and brought back our supper of boiled potatoes and turnip. It was delicious and comforting, and I ate it so fast I had to lie down afterwards with a stomach ache.

It was Friday night and my father would be going into town to fight, so I settled in for a night by myself. I spent the whole evening drawing on my slate from school until my eyes started to feel gritty. I said my prayers by myself and got into bed. Just before drifting off, Nora stuck her head in. "Are ye all right, luv? I'll be keepin' an eye on yer caravan so don't you worry, nobody'll be botherin' ye the night."

Tired as I was, I ran to the doorway and gave her a hug.

The next morning, even before I opened my eyes, I heard my father snoring softly, so I knew that he was alive. When I opened my eyes and took a closer look at him, I saw a little bloody bubble covering his left nostril, filling and emptying with every laboured breath. His nose looked a different shape. His left eye was swollen shut, and there was a dark red patch of blood on the pillow under his right cheek. My poor daddy, getting himself all bashed up for money for us. I started to cry. I loved him so much, and it broke my heart to see his handsome face all bruised and bloody.

I knew he needed his sleep, so I went over to Nora's for breakfast by myself. As always, she was glad to see me and had a bowl of salty porridge ready for me. She looked up and saw me standing at the doorway, her greeting warm and welcoming as always. "Come in, luv." Putting the steaming bowl of porridge down in front of me, she said, "Nye you eat that up. How's yer da the day? Is he all right?"

I told her I hadn't spoken to him yet because he was still sleeping, but I described his face.

"Yer da's goin' t'be all right. He's right'n strong and a good fighter. He'll do well fer himself at the boxin', y'know."

I cried in spite of myself, and the tears dripped into the porridge. I told her I didn't like to see his face all bashed up and that I worried about him.

"Don't you be worryin' about him. He can take care of hisself."

I choked down the last spoonful of the even saltier porridge, hugged Nora, and went back to the caravan.

On the way I had to pass Jeannie and Doreen, who were standing outside Doreen's caravan. They taunted, "So the wee uppity bitch is havin' ta go ta school."

They had probably been waiting all morning to say that. They stuck their tongues out at me and said, "Serves ya right ya wee shite." Then they both started chanting over and over:

"Kathleen McKenna's a wee guttersnipe.
Her face looks like a pound of tripe.
I wish ta hell she'd get outta my sight.
Nobody likes her the wee gob shite."

Oh, how I hated those two, but there was no comfort in giving them the satisfaction of a reaction. I held my temper in check and walked on by with my head held high into the caravan. My father, hearing me come in, lifted his head.

"Good mornin', luv. Where've you been?"

I told him. He seemed a little groggy this morning, which didn't surprise me by the look of his face. He looked as though he had taken quite a few punches the night before.

"Yer lookin' at me funny, girl. Don't be lettin' these wee scratches worry ye nye."

I felt the return of the tears that Doreen and Jeannie had managed to make me forget. I looked closer at his face and winced. " I don't like seeing your face all bruised and swollen."

"Ach, darlin', I'll be right as rain in no time attal." He swung his legs out and sat on the edge of his bed. "I had a good night. I won sixteen quid this time. I met a fella called Danny Keogan after the fight, and he took me out fer a wee drink. He told me that I cud double what I make at Jack Rooney's fights, so I'm goin' t'town next Friday t'meet him and find out a bit more about these fights. I might even watch a couple a fights Friday night to see what it's all about. It's a bit risky, but I'm willin ta give it a try if it'll mean more money for us."

I asked him what he meant by risky.

"Well, ya see, darlin', it's a wee bit illegal, seein' that ya don't wear boxin' gloves. The police don't like that, but men'll pay good money to see it. So I'm willin' ta give it a try."

Saturday and Sunday crawled by. It rained the whole weekend, so I didn't leave the caravan unless I had to. Sunday dinner was good. Wild Billy had killed and skinned six rabbits and given them to Nora to prepare for supper. Women and children had gone into a farmer's field and stolen potatoes and carrots. The combined result was Nora's rabbit stew. Although I felt sorry for the wee rabbits, it was delicious. It was one of the best meals I'd had since joining the camp, and it made the day seem a little less dismal.

After I had been in school a few days, it all became routine: I went to school, came home, collected wood for the fire, gathered whelks, cockles, mussels, crabs and dulse from the sea. After supper, I squinted in the candlelight to do my lessons.

It was almost winter, and very few vegetables were left in Farmer Donelly's field to steal. The market in town had closed, so there was no opportunity to nick anything from the stalls.

Nora and Archie were very glad of the prize money my father gave them every Saturday morning. It meant that they didn't have to go into town to sell their pots and cups as often or go rummaging through the scrapyard. At least the gypsies wouldn't starve while we were living with them. The weather was also getting worse with each passing day. The sea winds were getting stronger and rain was turning to sleet. Most of the gypsies in the camp showed their gratitude for my father's contribution by treating him with courtesy and respect.

After the first week, my father stopped walking me to school and meeting me afterwards. Without him to walk behind to shield me from the wind, my hands and legs were bright red and chapped when I reached my destination at either direction. The skin on my legs was becoming so rough it felt like sandpaper.

Walking up the long windy road to the gypsy camp was exhausting, and when I finally reached the caravan, I was tired, cold and sometimes soaking wet. Then I lit the candle, took off my dress jumped into bed and wrapped myself in the army blanket until suppertime. A nice hot bowl of mutton stew or a bowl of boiled cabbage and potatoes usually warmed me up.

I had been attending Flynn Memorial School for three weeks, and I still didn't like it any better than the first day, but it made my father happy, so I stopped complaining and went to school dreading each day.

On Friday, my father was going into town to talk to Danny Keogan, so he said he would walk with me to school.

He woke me up early so that I would be ready in time to get my breakfast. After my bread and hot milk, we set off. We hadn't walked too far when I realized I had forgotten my slate, chalk and jotter and had to run back to the caravan to get them. Doreen was sitting on her step with her mother and when she saw me, she stuck her tongue out at me. I sneaked a peek at her mother and ran into the caravan to get my forgotten school gear.

Doreen's mother, Sissy Connors, had only one eye. Her left eyelid was flat and permanently shut. Her good right eye roamed constantly, darting here and there as if in compensation for not having two. Nora said that when Sissy was fourteen, her brother had made a makeshift bow and arrow, and while they were playing cowboys and Indians, he accidently shot her in the eye. I guess my face expressed my horror, because Nora said, "No need t'feel sorry for that wee woman, luv, she sees more outta that one eye than the rest of us see with two."

It took half an hour to walk to school. We didn't pass many people, just a couple of horses and carts loaded with peat going into town. The people on the carts just stared at my father. His eyes and chin were still black and blue from his fight the week before.

"Good mornin'," he said pleasantly to each gawking face, whereupon the women would turn and look the other way. The men driving the cart usually said, "Mornin'."

At the school door, my father kissed my forehead and bade me goodbye and told me to be a good girl and learn my lessons. I waved just before he disappeared from sight. Then I took a deep breath and headed up the stairs and joined the procession of children walking down the hall to the classroom. Mr. Spencer entered the room and we all took our seats.

"Good morning, class," he said. We all said good morning. Time dragged on. I was bored with the repetitive lessons of spelling, writing and reading. My mind wandered, but I managed to keep up well enough. I was not good at arithmetic and dreaded the long afternoon ahead.

At lunch, all the other children either went home or ate something they had brought from home. I usually brought a piece of soda bread with mutton drippings spread on top and ate it while drawing on my jotter until the lunch hour was over. Sometimes I ate my lunch with a peculiar-looking girl named Peggy Ryan, who shared her jam or cheese sandwiches with me. Her straight black hair was worn in a short bob with a precisely cut fringe across her forehead. Deepset dark eyes looked like two dots of coal buried in her long, pale face. However, what she lacked in looks she made up for in brains. She was good at everything. Her arithmetic and spelling answers were always correct, and Mr. Spencer called on her to read often because she read without faltering.

When the bell sounded, we formed a line and moved with heads down, like a funeral procession into school. At least I had that in common with the other children. None of us wanted to be here.

Usually in arithmetic class I daydreamed and wouldn't get my work done, which irked Mr. Spencer and made his temper worse than ever. I had my hand slapped with his bamboo cane nearly every day, which he seemed to take great pleasure in doing.

Today after lunch, I was even less attentive than usual during the arithmetic lesson. My mind had drifted far above the clouds, and I totally forgot where I was. I was drawing a picture of myself riding a beautiful white horse with a long flowing mane and tail running through a daisy-covered meadow with mountains in the background. I didn't even hear Mr. Spencer's instructions to copy arithmetic sums from the board and hand them in within fifteen minutes. I heard only, "You have five minutes left."

I tapped Peggy, who sat directly in front of me, on the shoulder. "What are we supposed to do?"

Peggy made an exasperated sound. "Were you daydreamin' again? You'll have ta be quick. Copy these sums." She moved sideways so that I could see her jotter.

I was copying from her page as fast as I could until a dark shadow fell across the paper. A loud whack sounded as Mr. Spencer brought his bamboo cane down hard on my desk, making me jump. Terror and shame washed over me. I looked up into his cold, grey eyes filled with anger. He grabbed me by the shoulder, ripping the seams of my navy blue dress, and pulled me to my feet. He dragged me up the aisle and told me to stand on an empty desk at the front. I did this, keeping my eyes fixed on his scuffed brown shoes. He told the class that I was a cheat and a disgrace to the school and at the count of three the whole class was to boo me, which they did. Then all the pent-up resentment of having to teach a gypsy-child erupted. He shouted that he would beat the badness out of me and ordered me to hold out my left hand. It was always the left hand if you were right-handed so that you could still do your schoolwork.

With all his strength, he brought the bamboo cane crashing down on my outstretched hand, shouting over and over that I was a liar and a cheat, a worthless gypsy trollop, and a dirty little guttersnipe. Each time I drew my hand back he said that I'd get two more for being a coward. He was in such a fury. Spit flew from his rage-twisted mouth every time he yelled, spattering my face and navy blue dress. The fingers on my left hand were bright red and throbbing and so swollen I couldn't close my hand. I couldn't take this pain and humiliation any longer. Tears running down my cheeks, I screamed and pushed him as hard as I could. He reeled backward and landed belly-up on top of his desk. The bamboo cane clattered to the floor.

Mr. Spencer was livid. His face was absolutely white, and he acted as though he was possessed by the devil himself. He recovered and scrambled to his feet and picked up the bamboo cane. With a look of unabashed hate and disgust, he started whipping my legs mercilessly and through clenched teeth, screaming between each lash.

"Who do you think you are, you filthy gypsy scum? We don't want the likes of you in our school. It's filth like you that gives our school a bad name."

Each cruel lash of the bamboo cane burned into the skin on my legs and made me feel sick. The hot, searing pain was unbearable. Then his voice seemed to drift away like it was coming from another room. His face was getting dimmer and dimmer. The sting of the bamboo cane as it came down on my left leg was the last thing I remember before I fainted and fell off the desk to the floor.

Sounds and smells started seeping into my unconsciousness. I smelled leather and the crisp sound of shuffling paper. I opened my eyes and looked around me. Disoriented, I didn't know where I was. I tried to move, but white-hot pain shot through my body. My head throbbed. I touched my forehead and found a large goose egg. It all came rushing back to me. I realized that I was lying on the leather sofa in Miss Glover's office. I remembered Mr. Spencer beating my legs with his bamboo cane. I looked down at my left hand and it was red, swollen, and it throbbed every time my heart beat.

Scanning the walls slowly I located the clock. It was twenty minutes past four, and my father would be wondering where I was. I tried to get off the sofa, but I was too dizzy and my legs wouldn't hold me. Miss Glover told me to lie still, that Peggy Ryan had gone to the gypsy camp to get my father. She said that she was sorry for what happened and that Mr. Spencer had been under a lot of strain lately. She left the room and came back shortly with a cup of tea for me. A strained, worried expression etched her usually stern face.

"Drink this," she said. "It'll make you feel better."

I thanked her, but I was in too much pain to drink it. I just wanted my father to take me away from there. Placing the cup and saucer on her desk, she said, "Very well, please yourself."

The door opened. It was my father. When he saw me lying on the sofa, he looked puzzled and disbelieving. He came quickly over and knelt beside me. Ignoring the pain, I threw my arms around his neck and sobbed.

Cradling me in his arms he asked softly, "Cushla, darlin', what in God's name has happened to you. Who did this?"

I was crying too hard to speak.

Miss Glover was standing behind my father and in a measured voice said, "Mr. McKenna, Mr. Spencer discovered Kathleen cheating in her arithmetic class and became very angry. I do believe the punishment was a little excessive. However, this school does not tolerate . . ."

She didn't get to finish her explanatory speech because my father was on his feet and running down the hall towards Mr. Spencer's classroom. Miss Glover dashed after him calling his name and shouting something about being rational and not losing his head. Later, I learned that my father had found Mr. Spencer and had punched him hard enough to break his jaw. He didn't tell me that when he came back to Miss Glover's office and picked me up carefully in his arms.

Peggy was waiting outside sitting on the steps. She was crying, too, and said she was sorry because it was her suggestion that I copy her sums. I said it wasn't her fault and thanked her for getting my father. She said her father was a policeman and she would tell him the truth about what happened. I felt a little better, though I still hurt all over.

I felt safe in my father's strong arms. With my head on his chest, I could hear his heart pounding. The walk back to the camp was mostly uphill and my father, agitated and angry, had to force himself to walk slowly so he wouldn't jiggle me. He said what he wanted was to run, to put distance between us and that school.

"Forgive me, darlin', for makin' ye go ta that school. I only wanted what's best for ye, but you'll niver set foot in that damn school again."

I sighed with relief in spite of the pain and thought about the silver lining, my mother said, that was behind the darkest cloud.

Back in camp, all eyes were on us as my father carried me to our caravan. He laid me gently on the bed and covered me with the army blanket. I winced and cried out.

"Oooh! Please, Daddy, take it off quick. It's hurting my legs! It's too jeggy!"

He removed it instantly.

"Ach, m'poor darlin', I'll go ta see Nora and see if she has anything softer for ye to put over yer wee legs."

It had begun to rain and I lay still, comforted by the sound of raindrops hitting the wooden roof. In a few minutes, Nora came in with a clean but tattered flannelette sheet and a small, round metal tin.

She looked at my legs. "Mother of God, what kind of a monster could do such a thing to a child!" This was uttered in rage, but she spoke quietly to me,

"M'poor wee lass!" And to my father, "They call us bad, but we'd niver do this to a child."

My legs were swollen and covered in red and blue raised welts with some deep bleeding lacerations. She sat down on my father's bed and unscrewed the top from the metal tin. Very gently, she started to smooth something onto the welts and cuts. Both the ointment and her touch were torture.

"What's that yer puttin' on me?"

"Ach, luv, it's only a mixture of lard and zinc powder, and it'll help yer poor wee legs git better."

She shook her head and muttered. "In the name o' God, that man should be put in jail."

When she finished, she covered my legs with the flannelette sheet and took my hands in hers. "Luv, he'll pay fer doin' this to ye, I'll see ta that."

This was a cheering thought; I shuddered to think what she might do to old Spencer. Nora was famous for having the power of "the evil eye."

I slept the rest of the afternoon, and when I woke up, I had to pee. I swung my legs over the side, which made such intense throbbing pain shoot down my legs that I instinctively pulled them back up. The po' was under the bed and I would have to get it out some way. Among my four limbs I only had one good one, my right arm. I thought quickly, time being of the essence.

I reached under the bed and found the po' and dragged it to the middle of the floor between my father's bed and mine. I supported my upper body by placing one elbow on each bed, and keeping my legs elevated on my bed, I swung my bottom out over the po'. I nearly passed out with the pain, but in the end, I was very pleased at not having my father help me do something so private.

FIFTEEN

Nora came back later that night to look at my legs and rub on more of her salve. She shook her head. "God in heaven, but that man's made a terrible mess o' yer wee legs."

Sympathetically she stroked my brow and said, "It would be better if you cud sleep away the pain, luv. I've brought ye a magic potion to help y'sleep." She took a folded piece of brown paper out of her pocket, unwrapped it, and sprinkled a little bit of white powder into a cup of water. "Drink it all up, luv, it'll do y'good," she said, holding the cup to my mouth. I drank it all. It was bitter and I gagged. It had the consistency of wet chalk.

She gently pulled up the flannelette sheet. "I'll be back in a wee while to check on y' luv."

I couldn't remember much after that. I seemed to drift in and out of consciousness, and when the sound of Nora's voice woke me, it was Monday afternoon. I had slept the whole weekend.

Nora came in with some broth, which she handed to me after she inspected my legs. "Well, nye, my potions seem to be workin'. Yer legs look a wee bit better the day."

I still felt a little dopey, and when Nora left, the caravan was too quiet. I wondered where my father was. I couldn't get out of bed, and I would have welcomed his company.

Lying in the quiet, dark caravan, my thoughts kept returning to Mr. Spencer's raging face. Why did he hate me so? I'm sure I wasn't the first pupil he'd caught cheating. Maybe it was because he thought I was a gypsy? Why would anyone hate another person just because they happen to be different?

Deep in thought, my father startled me when he bounded into the caravan. He kissed me on the cheek, his green eyes sparkling. "Cushla, darlin', I have a wee surprise for ya."

"What kind of surprise?"

He told me to find out for myself. He said to reach into his cardigan and see what I could find. One side of his cardigan had a lump in it, so I stuck my good right hand in and felt something warm with silky fur. I lifted it out and sat it on my knee. It was a small grey cat with a tiny pink nose. I forgot about the pain in my legs and lay back down with the purring cat on my chest. I loved it already, and I loved my father for giving me this very special gift. When my father pulled the sheet over both of us, the kitten made itself comfortable curled up on my stomach and fell asleep purring.

"Now, m'girl, you'll hafta look after that wee thing. What are ye goin t'call it?"

I thought for a minute and replied, "Smokey, because he's grey, like smoke."

Nora was very kind to me while I wasn't able to walk. She brought me bread and milk every morning, broth in the afternoon, and rubbed salve onto my legs a couple of times a day. I shared my meals with Smokey, who learned quickly what Nora's shape in the doorway meant.

After a few days of staying in bed, the swelling in my legs went down and I could hobble around the caravan. My hand, although still bruised, went almost back to normal, though my fingers were pretty stiff. With Smokey to play with, no school to go to, and meals still brought to me in bed, life was not so bad.

The sun was shining, so I sat on the crate outside the caravan playing with Smokey. My father was leading a lame horse down the hill, when a policeman cycled into the camp. He leaned his bicycle against the wall of the farmhouse and walked over to Archie Mallon, who was sitting on a stool smoking outside his front door. The policeman asked him if he knew the whereabouts of a James McKenna. Archie said he'd never heard of him. The policeman seemed neither surprised nor satisfied with this response. He had seen the man with the horse and decided to wait and question him.

Upon hearing my father's name, I limped to the front of the caravan and sat on the grass.

My father led the limping horse into the camp and tethered it to a broken gate by the farmhouse and joined the two men.

"Mornin', sir, I'm Constable Joe Ryan from the Ballymacruise RUC. I'm here to inquire about a James McKenna presently residin' at this camp. Do ye happen to know where he might be?"

"Aye. I'm James McKenna."

The policeman coughed and glanced knowingly over towards Archie.

"I have a summons here for you to appear in court tomorrow mornin' at ten o'clock. You're bein' charged with assault by a Mr. Kenneth Spencer."

My father's hand shot out and snapped the summons from Constable Ryan's hand.

"Give me yer bloody summons! I'll be more than happy t'go ta yer court, fer it's not me who should be charged, but that bloody child-beater Spencer."

With concern showing on his face, Constable Ryan asked for a word in private with my father. They walked a short distance away from Archie. The policeman told my father that his daughter Peggy had told him what happened on Monday and that my father must be sure to show up in court to tell his side of the story. If he were convicted he could spend six months in jail.

"I'll be spendin' no time in jail. That bloody bastard Spencer should be thrown in jail and beat within' an inch of his life for what he did to my daughter, so to be sure I'll be in court."

Constable Ryan said we should arrive an hour early to meet with Mr. Montgomery, our court-appointed lawyer. He bade my father goodbye and told him he'd see him in court in the morning.

My father nodded. "Aye, y'surely will. Good day to ya, constable."

With a worried look and deep furrows on his brow, my father sat down on the grass beside me. He told me about his conversation with Constable Ryan and said that Peggy had told him everything.

"Well, darlin', I'll need ya ta go with me to court in the mornin' t'show the judge the state of yer wee legs. Do ye think ye can do that, luv?"

I could, but I asked how was I to walk to town with my legs still so bruised and sore. It was painful for me to get about, especially after sitting for a while, and standing up took time because of the throbbing pain.

"I'll ask Archie if I can take a horse and cart," he said.

I spent all afternoon and evening playing with Smokey. I would roll a little stone along the caravan floor and he would chase it. Or I would drag a little piece of string and he would try to grab it and sometimes tumble head overheels. He was such fun to watch, and it helped pass the time.

Supper that night was a hearty broth made from sheep bones, carrots, onions, potatoes, and turnip, along with a big cudgel of bread. When my father went into town earlier, he had bought a loaf of bread and some butter, which he hid in our caravan. The very fact that it had been smuggled made it taste even better.

I scraped some meat off the bones and mixed it with bread for Smokey. He ate it hungrily and then washed his face and cleaned his fur. When I got into bed for the night, he crawled under the covers with me and settled down. His little furry body felt soft and warm against me.

The next morning I took my longest excursion yet and hobbled to Nora's for my breakfast. When I got there, she was sitting at the table with a fan of large colourful cards spread out before her.

"Com'ere a wee minute, luv, and sit down before ye eat yer bread and milk. Nye, do ye have a sixpence?"

I did not.

"Go and ask yer da fer one, 'cause silver must cross me palm afore I kin tell yer fortune."

I limped, more quickly this time, back to the caravan. My father standing outside the caravan in his undervest, braces hanging loosely by the side of his trousers, peered into a small cracked mirror hanging on a nail. Frothy white lather covered his face with the occasional smudge of red. When I got close enough, I could hear the razor scraping up his cheek as he drew it toward his earlobe. Out of breath and without preliminaries, I asked him for a sixpence.

"Tell me, darlin', what would y'be needin' a sixpence for?"

"Nora's goin' t'tell m'fortune," I told him.

"Ach, sure I'll tell yer fortune fer nothin'," he said with his green eyes sparkling.

"Please, Daddy," I pleaded, "I've been waitin' a long time fer 'er to do 'er cards, and she's got them on the table now."

He took a sixpence out of his pocket and handed it to me. "Be sure t'cross yer heart with it before y'give it to 'er and ask God t'forgive ya. That wee woman's got a wee bit o' the divil about 'er."

I took it and thanked him and hobbled back to Nora's house.

Nora was sitting at the table staring down at her cards intently.

"Nye, you sit yerself down and give me the sixpence, and we'll git started."

I crossed my heart with the sixpence, hurriedly asked God to forgive me and placed the silver piece in her right hand. She put it to the side and placed the cards in three separate piles.

"Nye, luv, pick whichever pile is calling t'ya."

I picked the middle pile.

She put the other two piles aside and shuffled the one I chose. She placed one card face up in the middle of the table and said, "This is yerself."

She put a second card directly on top. "This covers ye."

She set a card above these two and pointing to it said, "This crowns ye."

The fourth card was placed below and she tapped it, "This is beneath ye."

To the right she put another card and said, "This is before ye."

A card to the left was followed by, "This is behind ye."

The cards were in the shape of a cross.

I was fascinated by her quiet tone of voice and the serious look in her eyes that had the intensity of a hawk. She placed four cards in a line underneath the other cards. I didn't hear a word she said about them because I was so captivated by her bewitching manner that I drifted into some mystical space of my own. She started to turn the cards over and tell me what they meant. She turned a card over and told me it was the Ace of Cups and another card that she said was The Star.

"Ah," she said, "this means ye'll have good news. Nothin t'worry about the day in court. It'll go well."

The third card frightened me when she turned it up, for it was a skeleton carrying a scythe and riding a horse with the word DEATH written on the bottom.

She heard me gasp and soothed me with, "Nye, luv, this isn't the worst card ye can git. This for you means there's goin' to be a big change fer ye. You'll probably be leavin' us soon and goin' home ta yer ma."

I was about to speak when she put her finger to her lips and shushed me. "Wait till I'm finished, then y'can asked me anything y'want."

She turned more cards. "Yer an independent wee lass. Ye have a sense of fairness in dealing with people. Y'believe that people get what they deserve."

With the next card she said that my luck would change for the better.

Then she was finished. "Nye, do ye have any questions?"

I thought for a moment and asked, "D' ye see in yer cards if m'da's goin' ta win?"

She paused. "Aye, he will," she said and gathered up her cards quickly and put them back into the drawstring pouch. I limped around the table and kissed her soft, cool cheek with real gratitude.

"No need t'thank me, luv. T'was in the cards."

I took my time walking back to the caravan, because I wanted to think about Nora's reading. I told my father what she said.

He smiled at me, "Well, darlin', I hope she's right."

Changing the subject, he grew more serious, "Nye, luv, are y'ready fer this? They'll be askin' ya questions about what oul Spencer did t'ya. It'll be awkward for ya, 'cause oul Spencer'll be sittin' in the front row lookin' straight at ya."

"I know that, Daddy, but I'll not be frightened with you there. I'll tell 'em what happened all right, and I'll show 'em m'legs. I'll not let them put ya in jail. No, sir! I won't!"

"Sometimes these fellahs have fancy solicitors and twist things so that the wrong man gets put in jail. If they put me in jail, Cushla, darlin', you're to take a bus home to yer ma."

He lifted his vest and showed me his money belt. "There's enough money in here to get you back to Belfast, and there's enough for yer ma to live on till I get out."

"Y'won't be goin' t'jail, Daddy. Nora saw it in her cards." I hoped she was right.

I went into the caravan and dressed in my navy blue dress. Nora had mended the torn shoulder so I wouldn't look shabby. I was still in a lot of pain, and the wool of the dress scratched the still tender flesh on my legs. Smokey was purring and rubbing himself back and forth against my legs and that was soothing. I picked him up and gave him a hug and told him to be good until I got back. I took a deep breath, pushed the army blanket aside and climbed slowly down the wobbly step.

Tom Sullivan brought one of the horses from the backfield and hitched it to the cart. There was only one seat for the driver at the front, so Tom picked me up in his arms and sat me down gently on some hay behind the front seat. Even though being lifted hurt my legs, it was my heart and not my legs that throbbed as he held me. While I had my arms around his neck, I closed my eyes and pretended I never had to let go. The prickle of the hay on my legs woke me harshly out of my daydream.

I stretched my neck up to see over the high sides of the cart. My father was talking to Tom Sullivan and he, too, looked very handsome all cleaned up. His newly shaved face glowed with health and good nature, and his brown fedora was pulled down at an angle over his right eye. He swung himself on to the front seat and peered over the cart at me. "Are ye all right, darlin'? This'll be over in no time atall."

"I know, Daddy, I'll be all right." I looked up at him with pride and said, "You look so handsome, Daddy, y'look like one of them film stars."

"Ach, catch yerself on, wee girl. Yer head's a marley." His voice was impatient, but he looked pleased.

He thanked Tom for getting the horse and cart ready and waved to Nora and Annie Sloan, who had come out to bid us good luck. He snapped the reins on the horse's rump and it trotted off.

On the way to town, the noise of the wheels rolling on the stones and the clip-clop of the horse's hooves made it impossible to talk, and lying in the swaying cart, my mind drifted. Thinking about film stars made me remember Belfast and the movies my brothers and I watched every Friday night in Jimmy McGraw's Fish and Chip Shop. Jimmy owned a projector, and every Friday night he would put eight or ten rickety wooden chairs in the small back storage room that he had painted black. He hung a white sheet on the front wall and showed classic silent movies. We watched the flickering black and white pictures while everyone in unison read aloud the words on the screen. It was the highlight of the week. It was in that dark little room that I first discovered Laurel and Hardy, Buster Keaton, The Keystone Cops, and my favourite, Charlie Chaplin. A thruppence bought us an hour of laughter and a brown-paper poke of greasy, vinegar-soaked chips. A heavy black velvet curtain pulled across the doorway sealed us in the happy vinegar-soaked world of silent movies. After the show, everyone walked through the curtain into the light, still laughing from the antics of the silent comedians, our lips white from licking the last drop of vinegar from the empty poke.

I remembered going to the Crumlin Road picture house with my mother to see *Casablanca*. I was completely spellbound by the beautiful Ingrid Bergman, and intrigued by the surly Humphry Bogart. My father, wearing his fedora and trenchcoat, looked like he belonged in that movie.

Memories of going to see *Flash Gordon* starring Buster Crabbe on a Saturday afternoon made me smile. If we didn't have any money, the manager of the Crumlin Road picture house would let us into the matinee if you brought a Keiller's crockery jam pot. Sometimes there were seven or eight children at the back door of the theatre clutching jam pots. The manager's wife made jam and sold it at the local market on Saturday. Usually the movie had already started by the time we got in, because paying customers were let in the front door first so they could get the best seats.

My daydream vanished when the horse's hooves struck the cobblestone street of Ballymacruise. My father tied the horse to a lamppost in front of the courthouse and helped me down without saying a word. Hand in hand, we walked up the steps and through the large, creaky front door. I could tell my father was worried by the way he was breathing. His nostrils flared as he filled his lungs with air, and his cheeks puffed out as he expelled it slowly. A man standing just inside the door asked my father's business at the courthouse. My father gave his name and said he was here to see Mr. Montgomery. We were invited to sit while he fetched the solicitor.

In a few minutes, a small man, neatly dressed in a black pin-striped suit, came out of an office and walked toward us with his hand outstretched. He had a very big nose, a high forehead and almost no chin, all of which seemed to exaggerate the size of his nose.

"Pleased to meet you, Mr. McKenna. I'm Alfred Montgomery, and I'll be representing you. Would you please come to my office so that I can go over your file before we go into the courtroom."

We followed him down a narrow, dim hall and into a musty-smelling office.

Floor-to-ceiling bookcases, laden with thick dark-covered books with gold letters on their spines, covered the walls. He told us to sit down while he got our file.

In his absence, my father leaned over and quietly said, "With a nose like that I bet that wee man could sniff out a criminal a mile away."

I giggled nervously and said, "Oh, Daddy, you're terrible."

Mr. Montgomery came back carrying a bunch of papers, clipped together. He set them down in front of him, removed the clip and began reading. Every few lines, he asked my father a question. My father usually answered, "That's right, sir," but a couple of times he said, "No, sir. That's not what happened."

Finally, he said, "My daughter, Kathleen, can tell you herself what happened. Nobody knows better what that bloody bastard Spencer did to her."

Mr. Montgomery looked at me. "Tell me exactly what happened on the afternoon of November eighteenth, Kathleen."

I told him every detail, including the fact that I had cheated in arithmetic class and how Mr. Spencer lost his temper.

When I finished, Mr. Montgomery shook his head, took a deep breath and said, "Dear, dear."

Then it was time to go into the courtroom. Mr. Montgomery gathered up the papers and told us to follow him. My father asked if I wanted him to carry me, but I said no, that I could walk on my own. I took my father's arm and we followed Mr. Montgomery up to the front of the courtroom where two tables were placed side by side in front of the judge's bench. Mr. Spencer and his lawyer were already seated at the table on the right. He glanced quickly in our direction and returned his eyes to the front of the courtroom. In a few minutes the court clerk stood up and announced the judge.

"Please rise. Judge George W. Davidson will preside over this hearing."

A portly, ruddy-faced judge wearing a white wig and a flowing, long black robe entered and took his elevated seat at the front.

The clerk told everyone to be seated.

The judge spoke in a stern, polished, English accent. "A charge of assault causing bodily harm has been brought against Mr. James McKenna of no fixed address. How do you plead, Mr. McKenna?"

My father stood while Mr. Montgomery said solemnly, "Your Honour, my client pleads guilty with provocation."

The judge directed Mr. Spencer to take the stand.

The clerk told Mr. Spencer to put his hand on the Bible. "Do you, Kenneth William Spencer, swear to tell the truth, the whole truth and nothing but the truth, so help you God?"

Mr. Spencer's broken jaw was wired shut so we could hardly hear him say, "I do."

The judge then directed him to tell the court what events took place on November eighteenth to bring about the charge of assault against James McKenna.

Through clenched teeth, Mr. Spencer painfully told his side of story. Every so often he stopped talking to swallow and wipe spittle from his chin with his handkerchief. Even though I could see how much talking hurt him, I could not find a shred of sympathy anywhere inside myself. Instead, I felt terror all over again. My mouth went dry, and I remembered how frightening he looked when he repeatedly brought the bamboo cane down on my legs. I slipped my hand into my father's to remind myself that I was safe, and that my father would never let anything like that happen again.

When Mr. Spencer finished, the judge said, "Thank you Mr. Spencer, you may be seated."

Then the judge told my father to take the stand.

My father walked tall and straight to the front of the courtroom. The clerk held the Bible out and asked my father to put his hand on it. "Do you, James McKenna, swear to tell the truth, the whole truth, and nothing but the truth, so help you God?"

"Indeed I do, sir," my father said with conviction.

Looking over the top of his glasses, Judge Davidson addressed my father. "Mr. McKenna, would you please tell us why you assaulted Mr. Spencer, punching him in the face hard enough to break his jaw?"

"Indeed I will, sir."

He told the judge that one of my classmates had come for him, and when he arrived at the school, he found me lying on the school secretary's couch and unable to walk.

My father's voice had been clear and moderate, but now it changed. "The man lost control, sir! He went mad! If my daughter hadn't fainted, he would've crippled her with the beatin' he was givin' her. She can't walk without help, and it'll take her some time to get over this painful ordeal, both mentally and physically. I would like, sir, for you to take a look at the state of my daughter's legs. Maybe then you'll understand why I was angry enough to do what I did. Any father would've done the same, sir."

At my father's outburst, Judge Davidson banged his gavel. "That's enough, Mr. McKenna."

The judge considered this request and then said, "Young lady, would you please come forward and show me your injuries."

Mr. Montgomery helped me to my feet, and I hobbled to the front and stood before the judge. I lifted my skirt, and I could see by the expression on his face that he was shocked. He shook his head in disbelief, then turned to my father. "Both you and your daughter may return to your seats."

My father hurried down from the witness stand and helped me back to my seat. Judge Davidson inhaled and then exhaled slowly, taking time to consider what he had just seen. He looked at my father, "Mr. McKenna, you are right! If anyone had done that to my daughter, I would have reacted the same way. All charges are dismissed."

When he spoke to Mr. Spencer, his face was red with anger and his voice was tightly controlled. "I think you should reconsider your profession, sir. Is this your usual punishment for cheating in class, Mr. Spencer? In all my days as a judge, I have never seen such brutality as this inflicted on a child by a schoolmaster. You should consider yourself lucky that the McKennas are not bringing charges against you. Good day, ladies and gentlemen."

We all stood up as the judge stomped out of the courtroom.

I hugged my father. "Nora's cards were right, but I wouldn't have let them put you in jail anyway."

He kissed my forehead. "Thanks to you, m'darlin'."

We shook Mr. Montgomery's hand and walked down toward the back of the courtroom. Mr. Spencer was looking at the table in front of him and did not look up when we passed.

Outside, my father said, "Well, Cushla, darlin', this calls for a wee celebration. How would ye like to get some fish and chips?"

"Oh, can we, Daddy?" This was unexpected. My mouth began to water at the thought of eating chips with lots of vinegar. "Do y'have enough money, Daddy?"

He put his arms around me and drew me to him tightly. "Ach, darlin', I'll make it up on Friday night, so don't you be worryin' about what we spend t'day."

We went to a pub on the corner called Mulligans. It smelled of stale beer, sausages and bacon. I thought it was lovely. It was warm and bustling with friendly, talkative men, some of whom nodded to my father. One white-haired man in a tweed coat called over. "What about ye, Jimmy, are ye all right?

"Aye, I am that," my father said, winking at me.

The man in the tweed spoke again. "Will y'be fightin' Friday night, Jimmy?"

"Aye, Davey, to be sure I will." My father was all smiles.

"What can I git fer you and yer wee lady there, Jimmy?" the barman called over.

"Hey there, Danny. Well nye, you can bring us some fish and chips, a Guinness with a Bushmills chaser for m'self, and a lemonade for m'darlin' daughter."

"Right ye are, Jimmy. It'll be a wee minute or two."

I looked around. Some of the men were drinking large glasses of dark beer, some were leaning on the bar smoking, and everyone's attention seemed to be on my father.

"Everybody knows y'here, Daddy. Is this where y'come when yer not at the camp?"

Absent-mindedly brushing crumbs off the table, he said, "I usually come here after the fight on Friday night."

The Guinness and the lemonade arrived first, followed shortly by the fish and chips. I sprinkled salt and malt vinegar over everything. The smell was pungent and wonderful. That first bite of the crispy battered fish and the taste of the golden chips soaked in tangy malt vinegar wakened taste buds long forgotten.

I couldn't remember having a more delicious meal.

My father agreed. "There's something about greasy, fried food that soothes the soul."

He drained the last drop of Guinness and wiped the white foam from his upper lip.

"Well, darlin', y'seem to be enjoyin' that all right. You'll be no empty skite when y' git that inta ya."

I nodded, but I was too busy eating to say anything. When we finished everything on our plates, the barman took our empty plates away and put a small glass of whiskey in front of my father. He picked it up and smiled, "There's nothin' like a wee drop o' the cr'ator to warm the cockles of yer heart."

He raised the glass to me, "Here's to yer health, darlin'," and drained the glass in one gulp.

He banged the empty whiskey glass down on the table and recited what he called a wee Irish sayin': "I've drunk to yer health in taverns, and I've drunk to yer health in my home, I've drunk to yer health so many times, I've nearly ruined my own."

Everyone in the bar laughed, and another whiskey appeared before my father. Several men held up their glasses. "Here's to yer health, Jimmy, an yer wee daughter as well."

"Thank you, fellas. *Sláinte*." Everyone shot back his whiskey.

Scraping his chair back noisily, he stood up and said, "Well, Cushla, darlin', we'd better git goin' b'fore Archie thinks we've done the bunk with his horse and cart."

A couple of men called out, "See y'Friday night, Jimmy!" My father waved back as we went out the door. I took his hand, partly because I needed help to to get along, but mostly because I felt so close to him.

My father gently helped me up on the hay behind the front seat, climbed onto the cart, and clucked at the horse. "Hurry up nye, Barney, and take us home." Once out on the road back to camp, my father started singing, but stopped abruptly.

He looked over at me, and I saw a melancholy look on his face. He smiled and took a long, deep breath. "Ach, nye, Cushla, darlin', I'll not sing any sad Irish songs the day, but lookin' at yer beautiful blue eyes I'll sing only songs with blue in them."

He started with, "Lavender blue, dilly, dilly, Lavender green, I'll be your king, dilly, dilly, You'll be my queen." He sang that one about four times and then changed to, "Blue moon, I saw you standing alone, without a dream in my heart, without a love of my own."

When he didn't know the words he made them up. The words didn't matter to me; I loved the sound of his beautiful voice echoing over the silent green hills. It seemed to me that even the birds stopped to listen.

After he finished singing Vera Lynn's "There'll be blue birds over the white cliffs of Dover," he said, "Nye, I'll sing ye m'favourite. 'Just Molly and me, and baby makes three, we'll be together, in my blue heaven.' I sang that wee song a lot when I was in India in the army, thinkin' of you and yer ma back in Ireland." He stopped singing. He was deep in thought, and now he was the melancholy one.

"I miss yer ma so much," he said.

He had a faraway look in his eyes, and his voice was wistful. I wanted to bring him back from the sad place his mind had gone to, so I asked him to sing "McNamara's Band," which he did. It was a lively tune, and he sang it so loudly it made me laugh. He sang all the way back to camp, and I was happy and content knowing that my father was not going to jail.

SIXTEEN

Back at camp a crowd was waiting to find out how the court case went. Archie Mallon spoke first.

"Well, Jimmy, yer not in jail, so I'd guess you've won."

"Aye, indeed, Archie, all charges were dismissed."

"Aye, and rightly so," Archie agreed.

Different voices said things like, "Good on ye, Jimmy," and, "Thank God that's over and done with."

My father shouted over to Tom Sullivan, who was talking to Ginny. When he heard my father's voice, he came running over.

"Well, what about ya, Jimmy?"

My father replied that all was well and that we'd won. Tom looked almost as pleased as we were and shook my father's hand and offered to take the horse back to the field for him. He held on to the horse's reins while my father lifted me out of the cart and carried me back to the caravan.

I held on to him tightly as he struggled to keep his balance walking up the rickety step.

He stumbled and cursed, "Jezez, that bloody step'll be the death o' me yet," but his voice was gentle as he helped me onto my bed. "Nye you just rest. I'm goin' t'have a wee yarn with Archie."

It was dark inside the caravan, even in daylight.

Smokey wasn't in his usual spot on the bed, so I called him.

I waited for a few seconds and called again, "Here, puss, puss."

I heard a muffled meow and knew that Smokey had come into the caravan.

"Come on, Smokey, up on the bed." But he did not come. Instead he darted out through the army blanket. I got off the bed slowly and made my way toward the front of the caravan when my foot slipped on something wet and slithery, and I fell hard on my bottom.

I almost fainted from the pain, but in a few minutes I struggled to my feet and cautiously made my way to the door. I pulled the blanket aside to let some light in. I still couldn't see what I had slipped on, so I tied the blanket back. When I saw what I had slipped on, I nearly boked up my fish and chips. It was a chewed-up headless rat. In the light, I saw that I didn't look all that much better. My legs were smeared with blood and my navy blue dress had blood and bits of rat guts on it.

I hobbled out of the caravan and headed to Nora's house. My father was talking to Archie and when he saw the state I was in, he came running over.

"Are ye hurt, darlin'? What's happened t'ya?"

When I told him about the rat, he sounded relieved. "Oh, thank God. I thought it was you gittin' hurt again. Go on in and Nora will fix ye up. I'll bring yer other dress over."

Nora was more pleased than alarmed. "Well, nye luv, that's what cats are for, keepin' vermin under control. That's a good wee pussy, he's earnin' his keep."

She poured some hot water out of the kettle and handed me a flannon and told me to wipe the back of my legs.

My father brought my other dress and went back outside to resume his conversation with Archie. I washed the back of my navy blue dress in the warm water and I hung it close to the fire to dry.

When I went back to the caravan, my father had got rid of the chewed-up rat and cleaned the floor, and Smokey was lying on my bed washing himself. I told Smokey that he was a good cat for killing the rat and then we snuggled down together and slept until suppertime.

After supper my father told me he was going into town with Tom Sullivan to make the final arrangements for his fight on Friday night. He kissed me goodnight and told me he'd see me in the morning. I didn't like being left alone at night. I thought of my mother and brothers, and I felt homesick again.

Alone at night in the candlelit caravan was frightening. I also kept thinking about Wild Billy. Maybe next time Nora wouldn't be around to rescue me. Silence scared me, but the crack of a twig or hushed whispering terrified me even more and made my heart pound. Sometimes I would sit on my bed with my hand over my mouth stifling a scream. Smokey helped some with his loud purring. He eased my loneliness and calmed my jittery nerves, but he was only a little cat.

I heard a woman humming.

"Kathleen, are ye all right, luv?" Nora's head appeared though the army blanket. "Yer da asked me ta look in on ye afore I went ta bed."

She handed me a steaming cup and told me to drink it. I recognized the smell.

"I don't like whiskey."

"Go ahead, luv, you'll like that. It's mostly water with a wee spoonful o' sugar."

I sipped it and she was right—I did like it and I drank it all.

As Nora disappeared through the army blanket and into the night, I heard her humming again. It was a comforting sound, which gradually faded as she walked away from the caravan. I snuggled close to Smokey, who was curled up warm and purring and fell asleep. The whiskey made me sleep so soundly I didn't hear my father come in.

When I woke early the next morning, my father was still asleep so I savoured the warmth of the bed, Smokey's rattling purr and my father's snoring. When he finally woke up, his eyes were sparkling with excitement. He told me that he had met Danny Keogan last night and that a boxing match against a man called Darcy Ferguson had been arranged.

"D'ya remember me tellin' you about Danny Keogan?" he asked me. "The man that said I could make double fightin' for him? Wait a wee minute, luv, till a git me fegs."

Reaching down to where his trench coat lay crumpled on the floor, he fumbled through the pockets until he found his little tin box where he kept his hand-rolled cigarettes. He lit one and took a long drag. He blew smoke upward, and it settled against the ceiling of the caravan.

"Cushla, darlin', you've been very patient with yer da, and fer that I am grateful. You've put up with a lot. I know you'll be happy when our stay here comes to an end, and I'll make ye a promise. When I've made two hundred pounds we'll go home. I want t'git us home fer Christmas."

I wasn't as happy as he expected me to be. "I want t'go home an' all, but I don't want you gittin' hurt. D'ya hafta fight? Can y'not find an easier way to make money?"

"Ach, luv, there's no work fer me anywhere around here. If there was, I would've found it by now, so what I'm goin' ta tell ye may worry y'some, but it's goin' ta benefit all of us.

"This fella, Danny Keogan, runs a different kind a boxin' club. It's called bare-knuckle fightin', and men pay a lot a money t'see it. He told me that I could make fifty quid a fight. Nye, that's a lot a money. So with the fifty quid that I've already won, in three weeks I'll have two hundred quid, and we'll be able t'go back ta yer ma with our heads held high. Then, I think we'll head off to Canada, Australia, or maybe even California." He burst into a chorus of "California, Here I Come!"

I was unconvinced. "But Daddy, I don't want you gittin' hurt. I worry enough when yer boxin' with yer gloves on."

He stuck his cigarette in his mouth and took my hands in his. "Cushla, darlin', I told ya I want t'git us home for Christmas. I'll be fightin' every Friday night so that means only three fights at fifty quid a fight. I can't turn that down, now can I?"

Before I could answer, he went into a coughing fit that made him get up and go to the door to breathe in some fresh air.

"Why would ya want ta leave Ireland? Does m'mummy want to go?"

"Yer ma seems all right about it. There's plenty of jobs in America fer plumbers and welders, and I've got ta have a job."

I was close to tears as I said, "I don't want to go to Canada or America or anywhere else."

"There, nye, luv, don't be gittin' all worked up for nothin', that's a long way off. Let's just concentrate on gittin' home to Belfast first. All right, luv?"

"All right," I agreed reluctantly and switched back to the other hateful subject. "Where are y'goin' ta be fightin'?"

"Now that's a secret. I'll only find out tomorrow night when I meet Danny."

I was about to speak, but he said, "No more questions, luv. I'm goin' t'be busy most of the day trainin', so you be a good wee girl and go gatherin' down at the shore with Nora and the other women."

My legs were improving fast. The swelling was down, and they didn't hurt as much when I moved them. I swung them out of bed this morning without even wincing.

Nora had my bread and milk ready for me. She smiled at my progress. "Well, luv, yer walkin' good the day. Yer wee legs must be gittin' better." I said that they felt much better and that I wanted to go gatherin' at the shore with her.

"Ach, luv, I'll not be goin' to the shore the day. I have two wee women from the town comin' for a fortune tellin' and a card readin'. The other women will be goin' though. If ye have a mind t'go, ye can go with them."

"No, I don't think I'll bother goin'." I knew that I wouldn't be welcome without Nora, especially if Doreen and Jeannie were there with their mothers. Instead, I went back to the caravan to think about what I would do to pass the day.

Every morning while attending Flynn Memorial School, a different poem by a famous poet had been read and discussed in English class, the only class I liked. After discussing the poem, we were given a choice of two subjects on which to write our own poem. The jotter and pencil that were given to me at school were still under my bed, so I retrieved them. I tied the blanket back and sat on the edge of the caravan with my feet on the wobbly crate.

Smokey jumped off my bed, sauntered over to me and nudged my arm. I decided to write a poem about Smokey.

Not happy with the first couple of lines, I tore the paper from the jotter, crumpled it into a ball and threw it behind me into the caravan. I repeated this exercise five or six times until a collection of paper balls littered the floor of the caravan. After a difficult start, my mind slipped into a daydream and words just seemed to come from nowhere through my pencil and onto the paper. I worked on the poem for a couple of hours, changing a word here and there and reciting it out loud until I was satisfied.

> The Hunter
> He sits in the grass, quiet and still,
> Ready to pounce, just for the thrill.
> His scared little quarry, ready to dash,
> Its tiny heart pounding, awaiting the slash.
> The cat inches closer, yellow eyes glaring,
> The terrified mouse decides to be daring.
> Jaws, with razor sharp teeth open a fraction,
> Ready to snap into fatal action.

The wee mouse panics and bolts for its life,
But its caught in claws that are sharp as a knife.
With one awful crunch, off comes the head,
The poor wee mouse lies quivering and dead.
The cat loses interest, saunters off in disdain,
Has a little rest, gets ready to kill again.

I liked the poem. I read it over and over and felt pleased with myself. I couldn't wait to show it to my father for I knew he loved poetry. I was no Rudyard Kipling, but I thought he would like it anyway.

It started to rain and I was getting tired of writing, so I covered the door with the blanket and pushed the crumpled paper balls under my bed. I would take them over to Nora's in the morning and throw them into the fire.

I crawled onto the bed and lifted Smokey onto my stomach. He was warm, and I fell asleep listening to his low contented purring and the soft drumming of raindrops hitting the wooden roof of the caravan. I was glad I hadn't gone to the shore.

Sometime later, my father came in soaked. Drying himself on the flannel blanket from my bed, he asked, "Have you ben sleepin' all afternoon, darlin'?"

"I have, Daddy, but before I went to sleep I wrote a poem about Smokey. Would y'like me to read it to ya?"

He sat beside me on my bed and said, "Aye, I would indeed."

He listened intently, and when I was finished he hugged me. "Ya know, Cushla, darlin', you really surprise me at times. You've a good wee head on yer shoulders, and yer older than yer years. If you kin write somethin' like this after that terrible experience at the hands of that maniac, as a boxer, I'd say that y'roll with the punches. I'm proud of ye, and I love ya more than words can say."

Pleased with his reaction, I hugged him and basked in the warm glow of accomplishment.

"Well, nye, luv, I'll go over an' git our supper."

Nora had made her delicious cockle soup. She had added a little too much pepper, so we sat slurping and sniffing. I laughed at my father. He moaned, "My God, this'd burn the mouth off ye!"

After supper, my father told me that there was going to be a bonfire and singing tonight. I told him I didn't want to go. He set his bowl on the floor and crossed over to my bed. "Ach, come on, Kathleen, you'll enjoy the crack and the singin'."

I told him I didn't want to sit around the bonfire singin', and that I'd rather be on my own than be with that crowd. He slapped his hands on his thighs as he stood. "Well, I think yer in a wee bit of a mood, so I'll be on m'way and I'll see y'later." He kissed my forehead and jumped down from the caravan singing "I'll be Home for Christmas."

I stayed in the caravan and read and reread my poem until I got fed up looking at it. I put the jotter underneath my bed and lay awake listening to everyone talking and laughing around the bonfire. I could hear my father singing and playing his mouth organ. Sometimes, I was just about to drift off to sleep when a rousing tune woke me up again. I finally fell into a deep dreamless sleep and didn't hear anything until the morning.

When I woke up, my father was already running around the perimeter of the camp with Tom Sullivan. This was the night he was changing over from a legal boxer to an illegal bare-knuckle fighter. I was scared for him. I hoped he knew what he was doing, for I didn't want him to end up in jail or get maimed for life.

I picked up our supper bowls from last night and walked over the hill to the stream. Kneeling down on the soft spongy grass, I washed them in the icy water. My bare feet and legs were cold and wet from the heavy dew of early morning, but this felt good after days of pain. When the bowls were washed, I looked around me at the mist-covered purple mountains.

Grey clouds languished so low that the tops of the mountains blended into the ashen sky. Leading up to the mountains was a maze of stone walls enclosing fuzzy white specks. Sheep dotted the Irish landscape in abundance.

I savoured the tranquility of the moment and thought to myself there couldn't be anything more beautiful in the world.

Compared with dreary, noisy Belfast, the countryside here was magnificent and serene. It would be paradise if my mother and brothers were here and my father had a job.

I splashed some water on my face and dried it on the hem of my dress. I returned to the camp cold but refreshed and headed straight for Nora's.

Nora smiled when she saw me. "Mornin', luv, are ye all right?"

I said I was and hungrily wolfed down the steaming, sweet bread and milk she had put before me. There were few redeeming features of gypsy life, but the landscape and Nora's hot, satisfying food counted as two. I thanked her and left in search of my father.

I found him sparring with Tom Sullivan in a clearing behind Tom's caravan. Both were naked from the waist up. Moving around in a circle, they bobbed and danced, trying to avoid the practice punches they were throwing at each other. They grunted with exertion, and puffs of white vapour rose from their open mouths. My father, sensing that someone was watching, looked around and saw me and went right on boxing. It was obvious that he did not want to be disturbed, so I went back to the caravan.

I jumped onto my bed and picked up Smokey and talked to him while I stroked his head. He was purring loudly and my mind drifted. I thought about Tom Sullivan's muscular back and the sweat that made his black hair stick to his brow. These pleasant thoughts were suddenly overshadowed by troubled images of my father taking a beating from an experienced bare-knuckle fighter. Fighting without boxing gloves was serious, and I was worried.

SEVENTEEN

I was daydreaming when I was brought back to reality by a familiar voice. It was Winnie Thornton, a quiet, middle-aged gypsy woman who lived with her husband Harry in the next caravan. She was telling someone where I lived and to go up the steps and shout in. Then the grey army blanket parted and Peggy Ryan poked her head in.

"Are ya there, Kathleen?"

"Peggy! Come on in! I didn't think your ma or da would iver let ya come to visit me here."

She sat down across from me on my father's bed. "They don't know I'm here. We got the day off school to attend a funeral."

"Well I'm glad you've come to visit me. It gets lonely sometimes. Except for my father, Smokey and Nora, I don't talk to anybody. Whose funeral was it, and why did ya git the day off?"

Peggy seemed to find it hard to begin. "Mr. Spencer died last Tuesday night."

I thought I hadn't heard correctly. "What did ya say? Nasty old Spencer's dead?" Peggy scowled, so I apologized quickly, "I'm sorry, Peggy, I didn't mean to speak ill of the dead, but what happened to 'im?"

With her eyebrows pulled down in a frown she said, "I heard m'ma and m'da talkin', and they said that yer wee gypsy woman, you know, the old lady with no teeth, paid Mr. Spencer a visit Monday evening and he died the very next day."

I recalled Nora saying that she would make him pay. I didn't know quite what to think of that. Could a gypsy spell have killed him? Her magic was powerful, and people who knew her made sure not to get on her wrong side. I decided to go and ask her about it when Peggy left, but I was in no hurry to have Peggy go.

"It's so nice to see you, Peggy. I think of you often, but I can't visit because I can't walk that far yet; and besides, I know that I'm not welcome in town, people thinkin' I'm a gypsy an' all."

Peggy couldn't stay, but she said she wanted me to know about Mr. Spencer.

"Ach, Peggy, do y'hafta go so soon? I'm enjoyin' yer company and it's nice to talk to sombody me own age." She said she had to and told me she would try and visit me again soon and maybe she could stay longer next time.

I walked with her to the top of the road, but we didn't say much. I was mulling over in my mind what might've happened to Mr. Spencer. At the road we hugged each other and said goodbye. I told her that when my legs got better, I'd take a wee walk in to see her. I waved until she disappeared over the hill. I headed straight for Nora's.

I was deep in thought when a movement on my left caught my eye. Wild Billy was urinating between two caravans. I tried to get past without his seeing me, but moving fast and quietly was not among my current talents. He finished then turned around to face me with his "thing" in his hand wagging it at me, and he said with a lecherous grin, "I hear yer da's goin' inta town the night. Do y'want me to come over and keep y'company?"

I turned abruptly and ran to Nora's as fast as my damaged legs could carry me. I heard Wild Billy laughing behind me. At the farmhouse, I brushed aside the heavy vines and breathlessly dashed in. Nora was stirring something steaming in the black iron cauldron, which hung suspended over smoldering coals. It smelled delicious and had the unmistakable aroma of mutton stew. Nora looked up. "Yer all outa puff, luv. Y'look like the divil himself was nippin' at yer heels."

"Wild Billy startled me, that's all."

"He'll not be botherin' ye again. Not if he values his miserable life."

"Nora," I said, not wanting to think about Wild Billy any longer, "I have some news for you."

"What is it, luv?" she asked, continuing to stir.

"Oul Spencer's dead. He died last Tuesday night." I watched for some kind of reaction on her face.

She didn't seem surprised. "Well, nye, that'll be no big loss to the world, will it?"

"Did you put a spell on 'im?"

She turned to me, raised her right eyebrow, and laughed. "Who's ben spinnin' you wee yarns?"

I asked her if she remembered Peggy Ryan, the girl that came to the camp for help after Mr. Spencer beat me.

"Yes, luv, I do."

"Well, she came to visit me to tell me about Mr. Spencer. She heard her ma and da talkin' about how you visited him on Monday and put a spell on him and he died the very next day. Is that true?"

She lifted the large black enamel ladle to her lips, tasted the stew, and added some salt. Not lifting her eyes from the stew, she said, "Well, nye, luv, I did go to visit that terrible man, and I told 'im just what I thought about what he did to ya. He told me to git away from 'im, and he niver wanted to see me again as long as he lived. I told him that he'd get 'is wish because not only would he niver see me as long as he lived, but that I would be the last person he'd see before closin' his eyes for all eternity. Call it a spell if y'like, but I think that some people are so affected by suggestion, especially from an old gypsy woman, that they scare themselves to death. I'll take the credit for it though, 'cause it make's me magic stronger in the eyes of the townies. They'll be comin' fer readin's and spells in droves. Don't you worry yerself, luv, he deserved it. He's dead and gone and that'll be the end of it. Good riddance, if ye ask me."

I wouldn't worry about it and deep down I felt that he deserved what he got. This strange little gypsy woman was my avenging angel.

I sighed with satisfaction and headed for the doorway.

"Supper'll be ready soon," she reminded me as I pushed through the vines. "I'm sure yer da's starvin', runnin around all day trainin' with that scallywag, Tom."

As I passed the Sloans' caravan, I heard Tom Sullivan's voice coming from behind it. He was talking to Ginny about my father and the fight. I walked toward the caravan slowly trying to hear what he was saying. He moved into the clearing between the Sloans' caravan and the Cains' caravan. He had his shirt on, and he was tying his wet curly hair back with a strip of leather. I stood close to the caravan by the back wheel so that he couldn't see my legs. I heard him say that he was going to the fights as my father's second. Ginny asked where it was going to be.

"Collin's Bakery in the bin shed at the back."

That was all I needed to know. I made up my mind to go. I would wait until my father and Tom left, and I would follow. I didn't care if my legs ached. I was suddenly ready for the walk into town.

Later, my father and I ate our supper without saying a word. He scraped the last spoonful of stew, and then set his bowl beside the candle.

"Nye, luv, I hafta leave soon, but yer da's goin' ta come back a winner. You mark my words, Cushla, darlin'." Patting his middle, he said, "We'll have fifty quid to put in our money belt."

I went to him and sat on his knee and gently traced his cheek with my fingertips.

"I'm worried about tonight, Daddy. I've seen what yer face looks like after gittin' punched with boxin' gloves. What'll it be like with some big hooligan's bare fist hittin' ya?"

He tried reassuring me. "Ach, Cushla, don't you be worryin'. I've ben trainin' all week, and I'll be movin' so fast, he'll not get a chance t'hit me."

I got up off his knee and he stood up. He stretched and turned to me and gave me a slow, mock punch on my chin. "I've got to go, luv. I'll see ya in the mornin'."

He kissed my cheek and left.

It was too early for me to leave. My plan was to leave after Nora checked in on me. It would be dark then and easy for me to slip away unnoticed.

I lit the candle and sat down on my bed and stroked Smokey, who was curled up fast asleep as usual. I hadn't seen him all day, and I imagined that he had probably tired himself out terrorizing some unsuspecting creature. Nora poked her head through the blanket.

"Are ye all right, luv? If ye need me for anything just come over. Wild Billy left the camp a couple of hours ago, so no need worryin' yer head about him. Just you go ta sleep."

"Thanks, Nora, I'll be all right."

"Good night, then, I'll see ya in the mornin'."

I waited for a few minutes and then put my cardigan and my Burberry raincoat on. I blew out the candle, kissed Smokey on his furry grey head, and left.

EIGHTEEN

It was cold and the stars were bright and sparkling in the black night sky.

My father told me that when you saw a rainbow-coloured halo around the moon, there would be a frost. I turned my collar up, put my hands in my pockets and headed down the road. The moon was directly behind me, shining on the road like a giant flashlight. The night was lovely, but it was eerie walking alone in the dark. Large trees dotted the fields on both sides of the road, and when the moonlight shone through their leaves, the trees appeared to be standing in black lace.

The silence was smothering, and I was afraid to breathe too loudly in case I missed a sound that might warn me of lurking danger. The solitary crunching of my feet on the stones was magnified by the stillness of the countryside. I thought of Wild Billy jumping out at me from the shadows, so I kept looking over my shoulder and straining my ears for any sound that might suggest that he was following me.

I wanted to turn back and wished I were back in the caravan with Smokey. But just as I was about to turn and run back, I heard footsteps behind me. I was so scared I could hardly breathe. I felt unable to move in any direction at all. Shaking worse than ever, I had to force my legs to take me over into the gully at the side of the road. Teeth chattering from fear and cold, I picked up a stone about the size of my fist. I was ready to defend myself. If it was Billy, I wouldn't give up without a fight.

I held my mouth tight shut and breathed shallowly through my nose. I heard the crunching noise again and strained my eyes to see who or what was there. If I squinted, I could just barely make out a bright spot bobbing over the hill. Someone was walking along the road and whoever it was, was just about ten feet away from me now, and he was getting closer.

The crunching noise stopped directly in front of me as if he sensed that he was not alone. He looked a long time in my direction. I clamped my hand over my mouth and nose and turned my face into the dark, damp-smelling earth of the embankment behind me. I held my breath until I heard the crunching of stones again as he continued his journey into town. I waited until he was a safe distance away and cautiously left my shadowy cover to peer down the road.

I could tell by the shape of his shadow that it was Harry Thornton, the quiet gypsy from the next caravan to ours. He always wore a light fawn-coloured cloak that had a smaller cape attached to the collar covering his shoulders.

I watched him disappear over the hill.

Relieved, I took a long, much-needed, deep breath. If I kept my distance, I could follow along behind Mr. Thornton and not feel so threatened. It would be almost like having a companion. The night didn't seem as hostile following Mr. Thornton, and mysterious sounds in the dark weren't as frightening.

I shadowed him into town, and as I suspected, he was headed straight for Collin's Bakery.

Few people were out on the street, but I kept my head down and walked close to the buildings just in case. A policeman walking his beat materialized out of nowhere into the glow of the yellow lamplight on the corner. He looked like an entertainer standing in the spotlight of an otherwise black stage. Quickly, I slipped into a dark entryway. He stood in the lamplight for a minute or so and then walked slowly past me and on up the street. After a minute, I stuck my head out and looked up and down the street and then ventured out. I had lost track of Mr. Thornton, but I was certain that I could find the bakery myself.

When I reached the seafront I could see, in the distance, the sign for Collin's Bakery in big white letters painted on the side of a large two-storey grey stone house. It had been a family home converted into a bakery and sat on a small rocky peninsula overlooking the Irish Sea. Its heavy grey stone construction protected it from the harsh winds and lashing rain that blew in from the churning water of the northeastern seacoast.

Fuzzy yellow lights glimmered through the mist from the building behind the main house. That must be the bin shed, I thought to myself. Noise from the fight would be drowned out by the wind and the roar of crashing waves breaking on the rocks.

The wind had a wet, icy feel to it as I walked along the stone wall that my father and I walked that first night we arrived in Ballymacruise.

Facing the seawall was a small fish and chip shop. The warm glow from the bright light of the kitchen and the occasional burst of a woman's high-pitched laughter were inviting. The delicious aroma of fried fish and pungent vinegar-laden chips made my mouth water. I sighed and tucked my chin down into my collar and headed for the bin shed.

I finally reached the bakery and walked down a dark entry towards the bin shed.

Two laughing men followed close behind me, and I flattened myself up against the wall of the bakery, making myself as inconspicuous as possible. Luckily, my coat was dark and it allowed me to remain undetected in the shadows. They stopped right in front of me, and one of them tossed a cigarette butt in my direction. It bounced along the ground and landed on top of my canvas shoe. It was still lit, and smoke drifted up into my nose and I had to fight the urge to cough. I didn't dare move so I rolled my foot and the red-glowing butt slid off. The other man took a bottle out of his pocket, and when he tipped it up to his lips, the amber liquid gurgled and sparkled in the moonlight. He passed it to his companion, who did the same, and then they disappeared down some stairs I hadn't noticed.

When all was quiet, I left my shadowy hiding place and crept around the corner of the bakery to the bin shed at the back. The bin shed was the same height as the bakery, but it was just one large room. Jutting out halfway up the wall on the outside of the bin shed was a corrugated tin roof covering the bottom row of windows, protecting equipment and sacks of flour stored underneath.

The first window on the left had twelve small frosted panes in it—three rows with four panes in each. Heavy mesh protected the windows from objects that might be hurled at them by bored, destructive children. I couldn't see a thing through them.

What was I going to do if I couldn't see anything? I went around to the other side of the building and discovered that there was a large window above the corrugated roof. I had to find a way to get up there, so squinting through the darkness I looked around to see if I could find something to stand on to hoist myself up.

In the moonlight I could see a dented flour bin lying on its side, rumbling as it rolled back and forth in the wind. I rolled it over to the shed and turned it on its end. It wasn't very steady and it rocked on the uneven ground, but it was the right height to get me up onto the corrugated tin roof so I hoisted myself up.

On the roof I discovered that the window had two broken panes at the bottom. It provided a grand view of the inside of the bin shed, and not only that, but the window well was deep enough for me to sit in. I could see the entire centre of the floor. Looking down through a haze of smoke, I saw that the shed was large and constructed of boards that had turned a silvery grey with age. Green hooded lights suspended by long cords from the high ceiling threw circles of yellow light onto the cement floor below.

The shed was filled with men sitting on top of large flour bins. In the centre of the room men were lined up, eagerly giving money to a man wearing a tweed cap and a bright red scarf.

Every time he took someone's money, he would stick the end of his pencil in his mouth to wet the lead, and then write something down on his large jotter. I recognized two men who were standing off to the side sharing a bottle of whiskey as the men from the entryway. Lurking at the back of the room was Wild Billy. My memory flashed back to him coming in to the caravan and putting his hands on me. I shuddered, trying to dispell the scary images and looked for my father and Tom. They were nowhere in sight.

The place was getting crowded as more and more men poured in. The air was charged with excitement as talkative, exuberant men awaited the evening's entertainment.

A tall, well-dressed man wearing a dark wool overcoat walked to the centre of the floor, raised his two arms to the ceiling, and shouted something I couldn't hear. Nobody paid any attention, so he tried again. "Gentlemen, please, can I have your attention."

He clapped his hands twice, then cupped his hands over his mouth and shouted something that seemed to get their attention. He pointed to his watch and then to the man in the red scarf and said, "My name is Danny Keogan, and I'm the overseer of this fight. This is yer last chance to place a bet with Dennis here. The fight will start in approximately fifteen minutes, so everyone please move back."

He turned and abruptly disappeared into the crowd. No one else came forward to place a bet, and the men standing in the middle of the floor started moving to the sides, leaving the centre floor empty.

In a few minutes, a very thin, scruffy young man, with a cigarette sticking out of the side of his mouth, appeared carrying a coil of thick rope in one hand and two tin buckets in the other. He gave the end of the rope to one of the men in the front row to hold and walked a ring on the cement floor, parcelling out the rope to men as he went, creating a man-made boxing ring. He put the buckets on opposite sides of the ring.

A few minutes later he set a wooden chair beside each bucket.

At last I saw my father and Tom. My father ducked under the ropes and Tom stayed outside the rope, placing two large jugs of water on the floor in front of him. A new, white towel edged with bright red letters on the edge was draped around his neck. I squinted to try and read the letters, some of which were hidden in the folds of the towel. But I could read enough of them for me to make out the name "Rathlin Hotel." My father was doing kneebends and shadow boxing preparing for the unknown. A second man appeared.

I swallowed hard. That ogre must be my father's opponent.

He was a big man with black, slicked-back hair and a pushed-in, crooked nose. He had massive biceps and a wide hairy chest. Standing about two inches taller than my father, he looked mean enough to bite anyone's head off who disagreed with him. He stared at my father and grinned malevolently, showing several missing teeth.

He shouted over to my father in a coarse, gravelly voice. "Hey, gypo, I'm goin' t'smash that pretty face a yours ta mush. Yer wee pansy friend there'll be carryin' ya outta here feet first. You'll be needin' some quare potent gypsy magic ta put y'together again."

Hoots and cheers rose from the crowd of men when he entered the ring. I was scared for my father, who looked too sweet and handsome to be fighting such a brute.

My father took a jug from Tom and poured water into his mouth. He swished it around and spat the water into the bucket. He bounced up and down on the balls of his feet and shook his hands at his sides. He looked nervous. He had deep furrows across his brow and he kept passing his tongue over his dry lips. My heart was pounding hard and, with the seawater lashing against the rocks and the booming in my chest, I had to strain my ears to hear what was being said in the middle of the ring. I was trembling from fear and cold, and my body felt stiff. I couldn't get my rib cage to expand enough to get a good, deep breath.

I clasped my hands in front of me and looked up to the stars. "Please, God, protect my father from harm. Keep him safe. He's such a good father, and he's only doing this for his family so that we can have a better life. So, please, please protect him. Amen." I felt a little better for that, but just in case, I kept both my fingers crossed. If I pressed my ear to the mesh window cover and if the men were quiet, I could just hear what was being said.

Danny Keogan walked back into the middle of the ring and introduced my father's opponent as Darcy Ferguson, "The Ballymena Brawler." The crowd cheered, and Darcy raised his arms and jumped up and down as if he had already won. My father was introduced as "Gypsy Jim" McKenna, champion boxer who'd come to challenge the undefeated Darcy. A tumultuous boo rose from the crowd. My father just stood where he was, bouncing and looking down at the floor. Tom patted him on the back and said something into his ear. My father nodded and continued to bounce. I wished I could be down there to cheer for him.

Mr. Keogan walked into the middle of the ring and once more held up his hands.

After getting everyone's attention, he said. "The following rules apply:

"Number one, only the two men fighting are allowed in the ring while the fight's in progress.

"Number two, rounds will last five minutes, upon which time each man will return to his corner for one minute for water and a breather.

"Are you ready?"

He looked at Darcy and then to my father.

Both men nodded and said, "Aye."

"Let the fight begin!"

My father started moving around the ring with his fists up protecting his face. Darcy lunged at him and threw a punch directly at his nose. He ducked and it missed. A collective OOOOHHHHHH emanated from the onlookers.

Charging forward, my father landed a good strong uppercut to Darcy's chin. Even from my elevated post, I could hear his teeth rattle. Outraged men were on their feet, shouting at Darcy encouraging him to retaliate.

That first explosive impact of bare knuckles hitting hard bone must have hurt my father's hand because he shook it a couple of times, then returned to his boxer's stance.

Darcy staggered backward. The blow must have caused him to bite his lip or his tongue. Blood poured from his mouth. He wiped it away with the back of his hand, smearing blood right up to his earlobe, and spat a bloody slobber onto the floor.

Outraged fans yelled at Darcy to retaliate.

He shook his head, then charged like an enraged bull. He pummelled my father's stomach with a flurry of hard punches, causing him to double over, protecting his mid-section with his elbows. At the same time he kept his fists up to shield his face. The men cheered and chanted "Darcy, Darcy," over and over.

The seemingly endless barrage of punches caused my father to stumble backwards and into the men holding the rope. Callously, they propelled him back into the centre of the makeshift ring towards Darcy, who took full advantage of the opportunity to land a punishing wallop to his unprotected face.

A dull whack echoed up to where I sat crouched at the window. The force of the impact made my father's head snap back, causing him to spin around and fall face down on the concrete floor. A slow, spreading puddle of blood oozed out from under his nose onto the concrete.

The bloodthirsty crowd was standing and cheering wildly. Men further back craned their necks to see the carnage.

Tom Sullivan tried to go under the rope to get to my father, but was held back. He had a scared, helpless look on his face. I was scared, too, and I felt even more helpless than Tom. My father was hurt and bleeding, but I couldn't do anything. I wasn't even supposed to be there.

Darcy was prancing in victory around the ring with his hands over his head. Everyone was cheering and shouting Darcy's name. He was certain he had won. Danny Keogan came back into the centre of the ring, but just as he approached Darcy, my father got to his knees.

Tom shouted, "Get up, Jimmy, you kin beat this fucker!"

My father staggered to his feet and assumed his boxing stance once again.

His left cheekbone, just under his eye, was purple. His right eyebrow was split, and a rivulet of blood was streaming down the side of his face and onto his shoulder. Blood was running from his nose into his mouth. He hacked up bloody slobber and spat it out beyond the rope. He wiped his mouth on his right forearm and lunged at Darcy. He hammered Darcy's mid-section with a flurry of hard thudding punches.

Darcy was on the defensive now in a crouched position. His arms were wrapped around his ample belly trying to cover himself. No longer able to get to Darcy's protected stomach, my father took advantage of Darcy's head being bent forward. He landed a punishing blow to Darcy's chin, which sent him reeling backward.

Darcy fell hard on his backside and was incensed that he had been knocked down. He bolted upright in a flash, growling furiously. He lunged at my father and grabbed him by the shoulders. My father's two arms shot up between

Darcy's, dislodging his grip. He drew his right arm back and delivered a solid punch to Darcy's left cheek. A second powerful blow followed, which snapped the big man's head to the side at an unnatural angle. This assault was followed by a left hook, which caught his stunned opponent on the ear. Darcy fell to his knees, holding his head in his hands. A roar of disapproval and disbelief erupted from the outraged crowd.

My father was dancing around the ring full of energy and with renewed vigor. His split eyebrow was still streaming blood. It ran down the right side of his face and was smeared over his shoulder and half his chest. He looked like a savage, painted half red and half white, that had just presided over a ritual sacifice.

Mr. Keogan motioned for the seconds to come into the ring, and Tom slipped beneath the rope. He put the towel around my father's neck and led him to the chair. Tom poured water over his head, dabbed blood from the side of his head and wiped the smeared blood off his chest. My father took a swig of water and spat in into the bucket. He and Tom were talking seriously to one another when Mr. Keogan came back into the center of the ring and shouted, "Round Two."

Full of confidence now, my father bounced around the ring. Darcy looked fierce, but he was clumsy and slow compared to my graceful, agile father, who looked totally ready to finish off this hulking brute of a man. Only a thin trickle of blood still seeped from the open cut on his eyebrow, but his right eye was swollen shut and black.

A voice rang out, "Come on, Ferguson, you kin beat the shite outta that fuckin' gypsy!"

In response, Darcy thrust a hard punch at my father's head. It missed. Darcy's eyes blazed with pure hatred. Like a wounded bear he charged my father, his two arms straight out in front of him. My father was ready for him. He landed a solid right punch to Darcy's left cheekbone, followed by a left uppercut, catching Darcy between his Adam's apple and his chin.

Darcy fell to his knees clutching his throat. He was frantically turning his head from side to side and his face was turning a deep scarlet. The angry crowd booed my father and shouted for Darcy to get up. Mr. Keogan ran to the middle of the ring and called for the seconds. My father didn't even seem out of breath as he sat down and took a couple of swigs of water and spat once more into the bucket. In a moment, he was on his feet again, taking deep breaths and stretching out his fingers, which were bruised and bleeding from pounding Darcy's granite jaw.

The men cheered when Darcy's second helped him to his feet. He appeared to be all right. He was coughing and spluttering, but he was breathing, and his colour had returned to normal. Mr. Keogan came into the ring and announced Round Three.

Darcy was circling my father with his arms outstretched ready to attack. Infuriated, he put his head down and rammed his head brutally into my father's chest, knocking him off his feet. As he fell backward, he slipped on a puddle of blood, which sent him flailing helplessly into the men holding the rope.

The sheer unpredictability of this action had taken my father by surprise. Darcy lunged at him and grabbed him around the neck, seeming to save him from falling, but no kindness was intended. Darcy drew back his head and thrusting it as hard as he could, head-butted my unsuspecting father hard on the forehead.

The crowd went silent as my father's arms went limp and his knees buckled. His eyelids fluttered and his pupils disappeared up into his eye sockets. He fell face down and unconscious onto the concrete floor.

The fight was over. Darcy had won. The crowd went wild, cheering and banging their feet against the flour bins making a thunderous noise. Wild Billy stood at the back quietly. He smiled, then left. I turned away from the awful scene before me and faced the churning sea. I felt sick. What if Darcy had killed him? Tears streamed down my face. What should I do? I was confused and scared, but most of all I was worried about my poor father, lying lifeless down there on that cold hard floor. I clamped both my hands over my mouth so I couldn't scream. And then there was nothing to do but turn around and look again.

Men were talking and laughing as they bustled around Dennis, collecting the money they had won. His bright red scarf matched the puddle of blood spreading out from under my father's face.

Tom bent over my father in the middle of the floor. He had turned him onto his back and was pouring water over his face and dabbing it with the towel. I didn't have words to describe my relief when my father sat up. He sat motionless with his head between bent knees. Blood, some of it fresh, was everywhere. Tom's hands and knees were covered with it. The white towel was dark red, saturated with blood from my father's battered, bleeding face. He looked broken and defeated. I wished I could go down there and put my arms around him, but I could not. I had to remain undetected. My father would only feel worse if he knew that I had seen his humiliating defeat.

I walked down to the seawall and climbed over it. The Irish Sea was surging and wild. Waves crashed over the rocks, spreading white foam over the beach. The icy spray soaked me through to my skin and made my teeth chatter.

The moon was high in the sky now and provided little light. I could hardly see where I was going. I crept along the seawall, trudging through deep wet sand. I managed to get far enough way from the bakery's bin shed without being seen.

The further I walked, the higher the wall got until it was too high for me to climb over. I trudged on, craning my neck and narrowing my eyes, squinting through the moonlight and the sea mist to see in front of me. Up ahead I could just barely make out the outline of stair railings.

I finally reached them and sat down and took my shoes off. They were filled with wet, heavy sand. I emptied my shoes and pounded them on the concrete stairs a couple of times. My hands were stiff from the cold, and the wind blowing off the sea made it hard to tie my wet sandy shoelaces. I crept up the stairs and looked up and down the empty road. I had walked along the beach about the distance of four streets so I knew approximately where I was. If I turned back one street, I could walk to the top and turn right; that would get me to the main road that led back to the camp.

With my chin buried in my coat and my collar drawn up over my ears, I headed straight into the bone-chilling wind. Once I turned the corner onto the side street I would be sheltered from the wind; that was something.

I had to get to the caravan before my father and Tom.

I had no idea what time it was, but there wasn't a sound coming from any of the houses that I passed. Most people would be in their warm beds on a blustery night like this. The comforting smell of peat burning, and the red and gold sparks that flew up from some of the chimneys, made me think of home, sitting in front of our fireplace with my family all together. My father would be entertaining us with a yarn about tricks the soldiers would play on each other when he was in the army. My mother would have made soda bread, and we'd be sharing a pot of tea. I longed to be back home. It seemed a very long time since I had seen my mother.

As I passed the last house and just before I turned the corner, I was abruptly awakened from my reverie by the wail of a distressed baby. I thought maybe the poor wee thing was wet and it needed its nappy changed or had a wee pain. It didn't cry long. Its attentive mother must have rescued it because the night was silent once again.

I turned the corner and headed up the dark, lonely road to the camp. Heavy clouds covered the moon, so I kept close to the side of the road and trailed my hand through the wet hedges. I didn't know exactly where I was on the road and hoped that I would be able to identify some landmark soon.

The wind whistling through the trees and the occasional flutter of thin leathery wings of some creepy flying night creature were the only sounds breaking the silence.

My heavy breathing from walking uphill made huff and puff sounds, sometimes louder than the howling wind itself. My feet were wet and cold and my legs felt numb. I couldn't wait to get under the blanket with Smokey.

Suddenly, Flynn Memorial School was on my right. I could be in the caravan in less than a half an hour if I hurried. Soon I made out the familiar honeysuckle bushes that stretched for about a quarter of a mile, halfway between the school and the camp. I trailed my hand over the limp, dangling flowers and put my fingers to my nose to smell their lovely sweet scent. They had gone a bit slimy from the cold, but I pulled one off anyway and sucked on the end. You could get a tiny drop of sweet liquid out of the bottom of the flower. That time of the year, in the hills, the weather got cold and miserable, but we'd had no frost yet to make the hardy little flowers fall.

A sound in the distance, like a car's engine labouring up the hill, made me stop and turn around. I'd never heard a car this far up the road before, especially at this time of night. It had to be somebody going to the camp, maybe Danny Keogan. He looked rich enough to own a car and maybe he was driving my father and Tom home.

I had to get to the caravan before the car caught up to me. I knew I was close. The honeysuckle bushes ended at the top of the hill, so I stopped trailing my hand. Stinging nettles grew in the culvert and I didn't want to have that agony to contend with, so I just ran as fast as I could with my arms outstretched and hoped I wouldn't run or fall into anything.

The car was getting close. I'd have to hurry to beat it to the camp. Its lights brightened the road for me, making it easier for me to see where I was going, but it was gaining on me. I could smell the petrol fumes, and when I looked back, I could see mist twisting and swirling in the headlights. I was puffing hard, out of breath, and through a haze of vapour I saw something glowing in the blackness through the trees. It was the dying embers of the campfire. I had made it to the camp just seconds before the car. I went through the woods behind our caravan and climbed in.

I was trembling. It was dark in the caravan, but I knew where everything was, so I threw my Burberry raincoat in the corner behind my bed and jumped in, wet clothes and all.

Smokey must have been lying on the top of my bed, because when I climbed in under the covers, the spot where he had been lying was still warm. I shivered. I wished I could have stood in front of the bonfire for a little while to warm up, but the car had stopped and people were getting out.

I felt Smokey jump up on the bed. He climbed in under the covers, and the sound of his soft purring and the feel of his warm furry body soothed me. I took deep breaths and tried to stop shaking. I heard murmuring voices and scuffling feet approaching the caravan.

The grey army blanket parted, and Tom Sullivan and Mr. Thornton helped my father up the step. There wasn't enough room for all three of them inside, so Mr. Thornton stood at the door and struck a match. Tom shuffled my injured father to the bed and gently laid him down. He removed his army boots one after the other and dropped them with heavy thuds onto the wooden floor.

Mr. Thornton handed Tom the lit match, "I'll leave 'im to you nye, and I'll come back t'morra."

Tom said, "OK, Harry, I can manage." He took the match and lit the candle and watched Mr. Thornton disappear through the hanging blanket. Then he returned to my father, covered him with the grey, moth-eaten blanket and looked in my direction. I snapped my eyes shut and pretended I was asleep.

Finally, my father spoke. "Thanks, Tom. I'll be all right once m'head stops throbbin' and me ears stop ringin'. Next time I'll knock that bloody bastard's head off before he gits a chance to use it on me."

I was relieved beyond words to hear his voice, but I couldn't believe my ears when he said that he would fight that hulking madman again. I'd have to talk him out of it somehow.

Tom took a small bottle half full of amber liquid from his back pocket and unscrewed the top. He put in into my father's hand and told him to finish it. I heard gulping noises as my father drained the bottle. Whiskey was a familiar smell to me these days. My father cleared his throat a couple of times and was about to say something when Tom spoke.

"Don't talk now, Jimmy, just rest. I'll see ya in the mornin'." He blew out the candle and left.

I didn't move until I was certain that my father was asleep. I removed my wet clothes and quietly dropped them in the corner with the raincoat. I would have to dry my things before my father woke up.

I turned my face to the wall and fell asleep listening to Smokey's soft purring and my poor father's laboured breathing.

NINETEEN

I had grown accustomed to seeing my father's face black and blue every Saturday morning. However, this morning after the bare-knuckle fight, his head had a different shape. There was a big purple goose egg on his forehead, his left eye was swollen shut, his cheek was bruised, and someone with big, clumsy fingers had stitched his split right eyebrow with black thread, leaving some ends dangling down over his eye. His face was a mess.

I reached under my bed and found my navy blue dress and a dry pair of knickers, and dressed under the warm blanket. My shoes were still wet, but I put them on anyway.

I walked over to Nora's for breakfast. The gypsy camp was quiet. Everybody was probably still sleepy from singing, dancing and drinking the night before.

Parting the heavy vines, I entered the farmhouse and went directly over to the fire. I took my shoes off and put them as close to the glowing embers as I could. When I sat down at the table, Nora put a bowl of steaming porridge in front of me, handed me a spoon and sat down opposite me. She folded her arms across her chest.

"Well, nye, wee girl. Where were ya last night?"

Some of the porridge went down the wrong way, making me splutter and spray bits down the front of my dress. I didn't know what to say, so I lied.

"I couldn't sleep, so I took a wee walk down the road a bit."

Nora raised one eyebrow. "Ya went inta town ta see yer da fight, didn't ya?"

I looked up from my bowl and into her piercing brown eyes. Dismayed, I hoped for mercy. "Oh, Nora, you do know everything. You hafta understand—I had to go. I couldn't stay away."

She uncrossed her arms and folded her hands in her lap. "Ach, well, nye, luv, I woulda done the same, if it were my da an' all."

I also hoped for silence.

"Please, Nora!" I begged. "Don't say anything to m'da or Tom that I was there. It'll only make him feel worse."

Nora avoided promising anything. "How's yer da the day? I hear that he nearly got his brains knocked out."

"He's not awake yet," I answered. "But if you've got some tea ready, I'll take it over to 'im and wake him up."

"Aye, certainly, luv." She poured steaming black tea into a white enamel cup. I thanked her, pulled on my still-wet shoes, and left.

I walked up the wobbly steps carefully, trying not to spill the tea. I placed it on the crate between our beds and turned to see how my father was. His hands were clasped behind his head, and his injured, bloodshot eyes were staring up at the ceiling.

I went over to him and put my arms around him. He winced and took his hands from behind his head and held his chest.

"I brought ye some tea, Daddy."

"Thanks, luv."

"Daddy, are ye all right?"

His voice was so sad. "Ach, aye, luv, I'm just a bit tired this mornin'." His breath had the metallic smell of blood.

Avoiding looking at him directly, I feigned ignorance. "What happened at the fight last night? Did y'win?"

"No, luv, I didn't. I really didn't know what to expect, even though I knew not to count on Marquis of Queensbury Rules. But I'll be gittin' me own back, don't you worry. I'll beat 'im at his own game next time."

I couldn't believe what he was saying.

"Daddy, please don't fight 'im again. Look at the state yer in. All the money in the world's not worth you gittin' yerself all bashed up for. M'mummy wouldn't like ta see ye like this, and neither do I."

"Cushla, darlin', this doesn't concern you. Just leave me to decide who and when I'll fight. Now be a good girl and take yerself off and give me peace for a wee while longer this mornin', all right?"

Gripping his chest, he turned painfully towards the wall and pulled the blanket over his head.

I gave up on convincing him of anything this morning. I retrieved my wet clothes from the corner of the caravan where I had flung them hastily last night and walked back to Nora's.

I called to her as I approached the vine-covered door.

"Come on in, luv," she called.

Archie was sitting at the table drinking black tea out of the same bowl I had used to eat my porridge. Nora was stoking the fire with a long stick. Red and gold sparks cracked and sprayed the front of her dress. I walked towards her and asked if I could dry my clothes by the fire and, without waiting for a reply, I pulled a chair over and hung them on it.

Archie coughed, "I hear yer da was beat last night. Is he all right?"

I tried to sound optimistic. "He's alive. He says that next time he'll beat the other fella."

"Well," Archie said, "yer da's a good boxer, so I wouldn't put it past 'im, but boxin's one thing and bare-knuckle street-fightin's another."

Nora was sitting on a chair throwing small twigs into the fire. I went over and sat on the dirt floor beside her. The warmth of the fire felt lovely.

"Nora," I asked, "do ye think you could put a spell on that fella that beat m'da ta make 'im lose?"

"Don't worry, luv. Yer da doesn't need a spell. Just believe in what he says. Nye, didn't he tell ye that he'd win the next fight?"

"Yes, he did," I answered, "but I'm sure he thought he would win this one."

Nora levelled her convincing brown eyes at me and stated confidently, "He'll be more prepared the next time, so don't you worry, luv. He'll win."

Whether or not I believed my father, I believed Nora. She had an uncanny way of knowing how things would turn out.

I sat chatting with her in front of the fire, turning my coat, cardigan and dress every once in a while until they were dry. When I put my dry warm shoes on they felt wonderful on my cold feet, and my cardigan and coat made me feel like I had been plunged into a warm bath. The heat was lovely, but fleeting; it dissipated once I moved away from the fire, making me feel colder than before.

I thanked Nora, pushed through the vines of the front door and headed past the caravans and away from the camp.

My legs felt better, not worse, after the workout of the night before. The only time I felt any pain was when I stood too close to a fire. The heat aggravated the fading welts.

It felt good to run, and I ran for the hills and the horse pasture. There's a wonderful sense of freedom when you're running with the wind blowing through your hair. I didn't want to stop. I reached the crest of the hill. I felt that if put my two arms above my head I could fly up to the clouds. I had never been to the top before, and I could see all the way to the sea. I felt warm from running, so I took my coat off, spread it on the grass, and sat down. I thought to myself, this must be what a bird sees from the air. I picked out my journey of the night before: there was Flynn Memorial School, and in front of the sea was the wall that I had crept along last night after the fight. The sea was much calmer today, and the water wasn't lashing up over the rocks. Almost every house had a grey plume of smoke spiralling up to the sky.

The sun, veiled in a thick layer of mist, was trying to break through. Shards of light burst from the glowing white circle, creating what looked like a doorway to heaven. It was beautiful up there.

I daydreamed contentedly until two little brown rabbits darted from a bramble and scampered down the hill in front of me, breaking the spell. I gathered up my coat and headed back to the camp.

The gypsy camp was still quiet. I thought it would be safe to take the short cut between the Cain and Connor caravans. My heart sank when I saw Jeannie and Doreen sitting on the front step of Jeannie's caravan. I pretended not to see them and kept walking.

They didn't say anything until I was directly in front of them. Then Doreen shouted, "Oh, look, the wee guttersnipe's got the curse."

Both of them laughed nastily and ran up behind me and lifted the back of my dress.

I hit their hands away. "Leave me alone, d'ye hear me!"

Jeannie said prudently, "All right, ya wee shite, but yer bleedin' all over yer precious wee dress!"

They linked arms and skipped back to their front step chanting over and over, "The wee shite's got the curse."

I wondered who'd put a curse on me, other than those two themselves, or maybe Freddie or Stevie? But no, although they were gypsies, they weren't old enough, smart enough or powerful enough to put a spell on anybody.

I went around behind our caravan to check the back of my dress. I was shocked to see dark spots of blood on the back of of the skirt.

A dozen thoughts, all bad, rushed in upon me. "They were tellin' the truth, I am bleedin'! Maybe old Mrs. Cain put a curse on me before she died, or maybe it's God's way of punishin' me for goin' inta town to watch the fight. Oh, God! What if I've got a terrible disease and I'm dyin'?"

I was petrified. I went into the caravan and sat on my bed and faced my father. He was on his back again and staring at the ceiling. Teeth clenched with pain, he grimaced and clutched his chest with his left arm. Supporting himself with his right he gingerly sat up and faced me.

"I was just gittin' up," he said.

"Does your head hurt, Daddy?"

"Aye, it feels like there's a wee man in there playin' a lambeg drum and another fella on a tin whistle tryin' to outdo 'im, but I'll be all right in a day or two. Don't worry, luv."

"I can't help it. I'm worried about you and I'm worried about m'self as well."

"What's the matter, luv?" His voice was sympathetic and kind.

"Doreen and Jeannie said somebody put a curse on me."

"Ach, Cushla, darlin', since when do you take any notice of what those spiteful wee cats say?" he asked impatiently.

"Well, either somebody's put a curse on me or I'm dyin'."

"What are y'talkin' about, luv? Yer as healthy as a wee horse."

I stood up and turned around to show him the blood on the back of my dress. "I'm bleedin' from me insides."

He shook his head. "Ach, luv. I know what's happened to ye, but I don't have the right words to explain it to ya. It would be better comin' from a woman. It's not a curse, although I've heard yer ma and other women call it that, and yer not dyin' either. It would be best if you were to go over to Nora and tell her what's happened, and she'll tell ya all about it."

"Yer actin' funny about this, Daddy. Why won't y'tell me what's happenin' to me?"

He sighed and waved his hand in the direction of the door and said, "Cushla, darlin', just go over to Nora. She'll explain everything to ye much better than I can."

I put my coat back on to cover the back of my dress and went to see Nora. I was confused and worried and wondered how long I had to live. I called through the vines like I had earlier and she replied as usual.

"Come on in, luv."

Nora was sitting at the table drinking tea and talking with Annie Sloan.

"M'da sent me over to ask ye about what's happenin' to me. He said that you could tell me better than him."

Nora said, "Sure, luv, what is it?"

I liked Annie, so I didn't mind her being there. I took my coat off and turned around and said, "Doreen and Jeannie said I've had a curse put on me. Who'd put a curse on me?"

Nora and Annie looked at each other and laughed. Nora shook her head solemnly. "I'm afraid it was God himself, or maybe even the divil."

Annie burst out laughing. "Jezez, wee girl, you'll have this bloody curse for the next forty years."

I was even more confused now at their lighthearted attitude. I thought to myself, I could have this curse for forty years or maybe even be dyin' and they're makin' jokes and laughin'.

Nora pulled over another chair and told me to sit down. She poured me some tea and asked, "Did yer ma not tell ye anything about this?"

"How could she, she's in Belfast?"

Another peal of laughter from Annie sent tea spluttering all over. Nora ignored her and asked, "So yer ma niver said anything to ya about what happens when a girl reaches your age?"

"No, she didn't."

"Well," Nora said, "nobody's put a curse on ye, and yer not goin' ta die. This is goin' t'happen to ya every month, and you'll bleed for about five days. This happens to every woman in the world. It's a very natural thing. It means that your body's ready to have babies, but you won't hafta worry about that fer a long time yet."

Annie chimed in, "Don't be lettin' any randy wee buggers mess with ye. Tell them ta keep their willies in their pants where they belong, and don't take yer knickers off fer nobody."

I listened closely and tried to make sense of what they were saying, but I wasn't having much luck. My mind was buzzing with all kinds of thoughts, but at the moment I couldn't single out one of them.

"Now, luv," Nora said, "you'll hafta keep yerself clean, and since ya don't want to be ruinin' yer clothes, you'll have to make yerself some rags. You know that wee flannelette sheet that I gave you when yer legs were bad, well tear that up inta strips." She held up her hands to indicate how wide. "Fold a wee strip up and put it in in yer knickers. Nye, you'll hafta change yer rag when it gets soaked through, so always keep a pot of water in yer caravan and when ya take it off put it in the water to soak. At the end of the day you'll have maybe five or six rags that'll need to be rinsed out. If ye want, ye can bring them over and dry them by the fire.

"Nye, luv, did I explain everything to ya all right?"

"Yes, thanks Nora. I'm feelin' a bit bewildered, but I'm glad it wasn't a curse put on me, and I'm glad I'm not goin' ta die, but it's not somethin' I'll be looking forward to."

Annie chuckled, but with sympathy this time. "Aye, luv, sure enough, there's not a woman on God's earth that looks forward to that time of the month."

Nora smiled at me. "Nye, luv, go and do what I told ye. Get yerself cleaned up and wash the back of yer dress."

My father was dressed and smoking a cigarette on his bed. He looked a little embarrassed. "Well, did Nora tell ye about what's happenin' to ye?"

"She did, but I'm still not sure I understand everything."

"Well, I'm not sure either, but at least nye y'know nobody put a curse on ye and yer not dyin'." He blew the smoke towards the ceiling and dropped the butt down on the floor. "Stamp that feg out fer me luv, will ya, an' throw it out."

I crushed it and squeezed it out through a crack in the wall and took the tattered flannelette sheet off my bed and started tearing it into strips.

My father looked over at me and asked, "What are y'doin', luv?

"Nora told me to do this and that I'm supposed to stick one down my knickers, so please turn around and don't look."

I rolled one of the torn strips up, went over to the corner behind my bed and, with my back towards my father, tucked one into my knickers.

Then I sat down beside him on his bed and looked at his bashed-up concerned face.

He put his arm around me and said, "My poor wee darlin', y'shouldn't be dealin' with this all alone without yer ma. I'm sorry I'm no help t'ya."

I laid my head on his shoulder and said, "It's all right, Daddy, I'll have a long talk with m'mummy when we get back."

Discussing this private matter with my father was proving embarrassing to both of us, so I tried a little humour and asked him if he was feelin' as bad as he looked.

"Well, luv, I feel like a two-ton elephant did an Irish jig on m'chest."

I put my hand in his and looked up into his eyes. "Daddy, please promise me that y'won't do that kinda fightin' again. Just go back to Mr. Rooney and do yer boxin', it doesn't seem as bad."

Without moving his head, he turned his swollen, bloodshot eyes down toward me. "Exactly what do you know about 'that' kinda fightin' and how do you know it's worse than boxin'?"

I'll have to be careful and not reveal too much about what I know and what I don't know, I thought. He must never find out that I was there and that I know all too well what happened to him.

"I just hafta look at yer face to know that y'got a quare clout from somebody's big bare fist."

I took my hand from his and spread out his fingers. His raw, bleeding knuckles looked as though they had been flayed.

"Y'don't git yer hands in this state either when yer wearin' boxin' gloves."

"I'm sorry, luv," he said. "I'm not goin' ta promise that I'll not bare-knuckle fight again, 'cause I will, and in two weeks' time I'm goin' ta fight the man that beat me. Only next time I'm goin ta win."

I started to say, "But Daddy," but he cut me off.

"Don't say anymore, luv. I'm goin' ta fight and that's that."

I was about to make another plea when the army blanket parted and Tom Sullivan walked in, carrying a bottle of gold-coloured liquid. I thought it was whiskey at first, but when he put it down on the crate I read "Mustard Oil" on the label. He said hello to me, and sat down on my bed opposite us. I went out and sat on the step with the blanket drawn across the doorway behind me so I could hear what they said.

"Well, Jimmy, what about ye?" Tom said cheerfully.

"Not bad, Tom," he said. "All things considered."

"For a while there, Jimmy, I thought ya had the bastard beat. It was bad luck slippin' on that puddle o' blood, givin' the fucker the chance ta nearly knock yer brains in."

"Aye, Tom, but he'll not be gittin' that chance again. I'll be ready for 'im next time."

"I've come t'give ye a rub-down," Tom said, "t'take some of the stiffness away."

My father told Tom that he thought Darcy had cracked one of his ribs when he rammed him with his head, and he was having a hard time getting a deep breath. Suddenly the picture of Darcy with his head down, charging at my father and crashing full force into his chest, was in my head. I saw again that terrible moment when he grabbed my father around the neck and head-butted his forehead, knocking him unconscious. Over and over I saw my father falling lifeless to the floor. These frightening images made me feel queasy. How could I stop thinking about them? They'd haunt me till the day I died.

My father improved remarkably over the next week. At first he could hardly move. He walked hunched over like a very old man, and when he coughed or sneezed, he hugged himself, wincing and groaning with the pain. However, his battered face was returning to normal. The area around his left eye had turned blue, then green and yellow, and in the corner of the eyeball itself was a starburst of red from a broken blood vessel. I wondered how he could ever mend in two weeks.

Tom spent a lot of time with us over the next week, and I certainly didn't mind. Sometimes I drifted off to sleep imagining him taking me in his arms and kissing me the way he kissed Ginny Sloan. But he never once looked at me the way he looked at her.

I also attended my father that first week of his recuperation. I brought him his breakfast and supper, I shaved him in the morning, and I watched him deal with the excruciating pain of his injuries.

Exactly one week after the fight, my father started to train with Tom again. He wasn't throwing vigorous punches like before, but he knew he would be ready and anxious to fight in another week. I was a mass of conflicting emotions, but each day my father grew more resolute as he got stronger. I was glad he was getting better, but I was very worried about him fighting "The Ballymena Brawler" again. I decided that I had a lot to learn about men. I couldn't understand getting beaten so badly that you could hardly walk or see out of one of your eyes, and still want to get back into the ring and do the same thing again. But, having survived my first week of womanhood, I supposed that men could be figured out in time.

TWENTY

It was cold and rainy, and I spent too much time on my own in our dreary, dilapidated caravan. My father was busy training and getting in shape for his next fight, and I felt homesick and lonely.

Smokey was nice to have around, but he couldn't talk to me. I didn't want to go over to Nora's too often. She had her own friends and her cards and stones, and sometimes women from the town would visit her for a fortune-telling and a tarot card reading. I desperately wanted to go home. According to my father, Christmas was three weeks away. It seemed like forever.

I thought that a visit to Peggy Ryan would cheer me up. Besides my father and Tom and Nora, she was my only friend, and it had been weeks since she had come to tell me about Mr. Spencer's death.

I ran over to Nora's to find out what time it was. If anybody could tell me the time, she could. She had a shoebox full of watches that at one time probably belonged to the good people of Ballymacruise.

It was a quarter to four. Peggy would be out of school in fifteen minutes and home by the time I got to her house. I washed my face, brushed and plaited my hair, put my Burberry raincoat on and left. The very thought of talking to my friend lifted my spirits.

It was a short two-minute walk through the woods behind the caravan to the main road. It was remarkably different in daylight. No dark shadows with imagined evil lurking within. Except for the constant bleating of sheep echoing through the countryside, the daytime sounds were the same.

I dragged my hand through the soft, limp flowers of the honeysuckle bushes and again filled my nostrils with their sweet fragrance. Escaping the confines of the small, dark caravan and getting away from the gypsy camp gave me a sense of freedom.

As I drew near the school, I heard laughter and shouting. Some boys were kicking a scuffed, leather football to each other. I felt apprehensive passing them. Illogically, I felt guilty as though I had caused Mr. Spencer's death. Everyone believed a gypsy curse had killed him for what he did to me.

In a way, my father and I had become gypsies, not by choice but for survival, and I felt I belonged with them more than the townspeople.

The boys, all younger than I was, stopped playing their game as I passed. The laughter and shouting faded to silence. I felt their eyes on me, and I became self-conscious. Looking intently at the road in front of me, I walked quickly past them.

Suddenly, a stone hit my left temple. I touched the spot where it had struck. When I took my hand away, there was blood on my fingers.

A barrage of stones followed. I started to run and put my left arm up to protect my face.

"Git away from here, ya dirty gypsy skite!"

A barrage of stones followed. Each time a boy hurled a stone he shouted, "gypsy skite, gypsy skite." I started running as fast as I could.

I was terrified.

Out of the corner of my eye I could see someone running beside me. Tears were streaming down my cheeks, blurring my vision. It was a boy about a head taller than me and about my age. I blinked a couple of times to clear my eyes and lashed out at him. I tried to pound him with my fist and push him away, but he paid no attention. He was holding a book up at the side of my face and shouting back at the rowdy boys, "Quit throwin' them stones, ya wee fuckers, or you'll be sorry!"

I finally realized then that he was on my side and trying to protect me from the stones. He stopped to pick up a stone and hurled it back at them.

Dashing in front of me, he shouted, "Come on!" Then he grabbed my hand and pulled me along behind him. We ran hand in hand until we reached the bottom of the hill, and turned off the road onto a dirt path that led to the ruins of an old stone church. We stopped running when we were well out of sight and sat down on a row of square stones that had once been part of the church.

"Are y'all right? he asked. "Yer head's bleedin' a bit, but not much."

I looked down at my feet while I caught my breath. I knew this boy. He was Quinton O'Hara, and he had been in Mr. Spencer's class. I had never spoken to him, but sometimes out of the corner of my eye I had seen him looking at me.

"I'm all right," I answered. "But I don't understand why they hate me. I've niver done nothin' t'them. It wasn't my choice t'go t'their stupid school and get beaten by their divil of a master, who's dead and gone and I'm glad."

Too late, I realized that this might not have been a wise thing to say. I looked at him sideways for a reaction. There was none, and alarm and fear gave way to puzzlement. "Why did you help me back there, and why don't you hate me like the rest a them?"

He looked at me with blue-green eyes that sparkled through golden lashes. "Maybe it's because I like you. You're different. You're smart and you're pretty and when that fucker Spencer was beatin' ya, I felt every stroke go through m'heart for ya."

My puzzlement deepened. I thought for a moment. "Well, Quinton, I didn't think anybody in that whole class cared what happened to me except Peggy Ryan."

"Well, I did, and would y'please call me Quin, that's what m'friends call me."

I answered with an embarrassed giggle, "All right, Quin."

Neither of us spoke for a minute, and I looked at his hands. They were red and chapped and I remembered that when he pulled me away from the flying stones his skin felt rough, like sandpaper.

I broke the silence. "Why's yer hands so red? They look sore."

"Ach, sure, they're not sore. M'da's a winda washer and I go and help 'im sometimes. M'hands are always in water, and the cold makes them red and rough. Sure m'da's are the same. I kin tell ya this, Kate, I'll not be a winda washer when I grow up. There's better and easier ways to make money than that." He paused. "Well, Kate, I hear yer da's a boxer."

Very deliberately, I said, "My name is not Kate, nobody iver calls me that. M'name's Kathleen."

"All right, Kathleen, but I'll call ya Kate just the same."

In a haughty voice I replied, "Then I probably won't answer ya."

"Oh yes y'will, Kate." And we both smiled.

He was a handsome boy with golden blond hair and a lovely smile.

"How do you know that my father's a boxer?"

"Everybody in town knows about 'Gypsy Jim' McKenna. M'da's seen ivery one of his fights, includin' the bare-fist one 'e lost a week ago Friday night when he nearly got his brains knocked in. M'da says that big brute 'e was fightin's no boxer, just a street brawler with a mean streak and a wicked temper."

I paused only a second, then trying to impress him, I boasted. "I saw that fight. I sneaked inta town to Collin's Bakery and saw the whole thing."

Quin was impressed. He looked at me, his blue-green eyes flashing with excitement, and he asked, "You did what! How did y'manage that without bein' seen?"

I raised my right eyebrow like Nora, and with an impish grin replied, "I used magic. I'm a gypsy, y'know."

"Ach," he said impatiently, "catch yerself on, but really nye, how did y'manage it?"

"Well, the truth is, I heard m'father's friend Tom tellin' his girl where it was, so I just waited till it was dark and sneaked inta town."

"You're a quare, sleekit wee girl, and I like that. The next time I'm goin' with ya. So, when's the next one?"

A dark cloud seemed to roll across the sun. "It's supposed to take place on Friday, and that's only two days away, but I don't think my father's well enough to fight."

Quin sounded remarkably reassuring for someone who had never met my father and had until recently not spoken one word to me. "Well, Kate, don't you worry. He'll be prepared for 'im next time. He'll know when to duck and when to get the hell outta his way. So, just after dark, I'll meet ye at the top o' the road, just before it turns into the gypsy camp. M'da'll be at the fight, and m'ma takes in washin', and Friday night's a busy night for 'er, so she won't be missin' me."

"All right," I agreed.

I didn't know how long we sat talking, but I really enjoyed being with Quin. I had made a new friend, and I felt lighthearted and happy for the first time in a long while. We sat quietly for a few minutes, and then I thought I'd better get on my way to Peggy's. I stood up, and he followed. I looked up at him. The sun was directly behind his head turning his hair into a fuzzy golden halo.

"I'll see ya Friday night then, and I'd like to thank ya for savin' me from those awful wee brutes. I don't know what would've happened to me if y'hadn't been there. I might've been stoned to death."

He smiled. "Ach, y'would've used yer gypsy magic and disappeared or somethin'."

I grinned back. "Goodbye, Quin, I'll see ya Friday night."

"Goodbye, Kate," he said and ran up to the road. He turned and looked back and waved, and I waved back. A nice warm feeling of happiness surged over me. He said that he liked me and that I was pretty. I felt like a princess in a fairy tale, and the day looked brighter than I had thought possible only a few hours before.

I continued on to Peggy Ryan's house, which wasn't far from the ruined church. I felt apprehensive when I reached her house. The black, wrought-iron gate gave a hideous screech when I pushed it open, and I replaced it with great care.

Standing uncomfortably on her doorstep, I wondered whether I should turn back. I'd had enough animosity for one day, but the good had an edge over the bad, and I didn't want to spoil it. I'd never met Peggy's mother and didn't know how she would react to my arriving on her doorstep.

As far as the townspeople were concerned, I was a gypsy and not to be trusted. I decided, however, that my need to see Peggy overcame my fear of her mother's disapproval, so I lifted the door knocker and knocked twice. I held my breath for a few seconds, ready to bolt if her mother appeared, but Peggy answered the door, and she smiled broadly when she saw me.

She pulled me through the open door. "Come on in, Kathleen, I'm glad to see ya. I've been thinking about ya."

I relaxed a bit and took a deep breath. She brought me into the parlour where a fire sparked and crackled in the middle of the room.

Staring at me, she asked, "What have y'done to yer head? Did ya fall?"

I didn't want to tell her about the boys throwing stones at me, so I just said that I had scraped it on a stone wall when I was running. I had something else on my mind.

"Will yer mother mind that I'm in yer house?"

"No, I don't think so. M'mommy's not like that, but wait here and I'll go t'the scullery and tell her yer here."

I could hear them talking, but I couldn't make out what was being said over the roar of the fire. A few minutes later, Peggy came back into the parlour with her mother.

I stood up. "Hello, Mrs. Ryan."

Holding out her hand to me, she said, "Hello, Kathleen, I'm pleased t'meet ya. Peggy's told me a lot about ya." She paused briefly. "Please sit down. Would y'like a wee cup a tea to warm y'up, luv?"

I couldn't believe how friendly and pleasant she was. I breathed again and nodded with real gratitude. She had a pretty face and brown, wavy shoulder-length hair, held back off her face by a bronze-coloured clip at the side. It was obvious that Peggy wasn't fortunate enough to take after her mother, but she didn't look like her father either.

While Mrs. Ryan made tea, Peggy and I sat in front of the fire. I loved the homey feeling of the room—the pictures of relatives on the wall, lacy curtains on the windows, the velvety feel of the carpet, and the warm, amber glow of the lamp in the corner. This was heaven compared to our cold, dark, wretched caravan. Unexpectedly, these totally opposite surroundings made me wish I hadn't come. Waves of homesickness battered at my heart, making me feel more fragile than ever, and I longed to be where my own mother was making me tea.

As if trying to escape the heaviness of my mood, my mind drifted far away, to my own home in Belfast. Flooding my memory were the sounds and smells of our little house on the corner of Nore Street. It was very similar to this one. Two bedrooms upstairs and a parlour and a scullery downstairs.

Eight-foot brick walls surrounded our yard at the back. There wasn't a blade of grass anywhere to be seen. Sometimes green, velvety moss grew on the damp yard walls, and occasionally a little daisy managed to survive on the tiny patch of green. At the bottom of the yard was an open-front shed, which covered the washtub, scrub board and mangle. In one corner was a separate stall with a door that gave privacy to our toilet. Crossing from wall to wall were ropes to hang clothes on to dry.

My job when I got home from school was to cut the Belfast Telegraph into wee squares and poke a hole in the corner with the sharp point of the scissors. Then I'd thread a cord through the hole so that the newspaper squares could hang on a nail in the toilet. When getting washed before going to bed at night, my mother would take special care to wash the black smudges off our backsides from wiping them with the newsprint.

The whistle of the teakettle broke the spell.

Peggy must have sensed that my mind had drifted far away because she didn't say a word until I sighed and smiled at her. She had been tracing the pattern in the carpet with her finger and now she asked, "How's yer daddy? I heard that he got beat pretty bad in his last fight."

I was astonished. Even Peggy knew about the fight. "How did y'come to know about that?"

"Well, ya know m'da's a policeman, Kathleen, and he knows everything that goes on in this wee town. Even though that kind o' boxin's illegal, the police know it goes on here. M'da says there's little enough to do here on a Friday night. Yer da's made a quare name for himself with his boxin'."

Just then Constable Ryan came in wearing his uniform. Peggy's father was a nice man, but that dark blue uniform and his shiny badge made me want to run.

He hung his hat and overcoat on a coat hook behind the front door. Smiling, he walked over to the front of the fire. He bent down and kissed Peggy on the cheek.

"Hello, luv, I see you've got a visitor." Then looking down at me he said, "Well, Kathleen McKenna, what about ya, are ye all right?"

"I'm doin' all right, thank you, Constable Ryan."

"And how's yer da? I hear he took quite a beatin' a fortnight back."

Cautiously I answered the policeman's question. "He's better, thanks."

He might have asked more, but his wife appeared with a tray of tea and biscuits and asked Peggy to pull out the largest table from a nest of tables stacked neatly against the wall. Peggy did as she was told and placed the table in front of the worn blue sofa.

As Mrs. Ryan placed the tray on the table she looked up at Constable Ryan and said, "Hello, luv, I didn't hear y'come in. Would y'like a wee cup o' tea." He left to get another cup. Peggy handed me a dainty gold-rimmed cup with pink roses and told me to help myself to the milk, sugar and biscuits. Constable Ryan returned, and we all sat around the fire drinking tea and munching biscuits.

It was wonderful—it had been a long time since I had good tea in a lovely cup and in such a loving family atmosphere. The biscuits were crunchy and delicious and obviously homemade.

It was all very nice, but looming over me like a big black cloud was the gloomy image of the cold, rat-infested gypsy caravan. A wave of panic swept over me, and I had to choke back tears. I put my cup back on the tray and stood up. I thanked Mr. and Mrs Ryan and told them I had to get home for supper and that my father would be worried about me. Mrs. Ryan invited me to stay for supper, but I said no, thank you. My heart was thumping hard and fast in my chest. I had to get out. Peggy brought me my coat.

On the way to the door she asked, "What's the matter, Kathleen? Did we say somethin' to offend ye?"

"Oh no, Peggy not at all. Yer mother and father are very nice, and yer home is lovely. I just feel sad knowing what I have to go back to at the gypsy camp."

Peggy sighed. "Thank you for visiting me, Kathleen, and I hope you'll come back again. You're always welcome."

"I will, Peggy, now that I've met yer mother, and she doesn't seem to mind that I live with the gypsies." My feeling of panic left while standing at the door. I gave Peggy a grateful hug and hurried out into the street.

Delicious smells of fried onions, bacon and homemade bread drifted out of houses I passed. I felt more homesick than ever.

TWENTY-ONE

When I reached the caravan, my father was sitting outside on the step wearing a new dark green cardigan. Smoke spiraled upward from a cigarette in his right hand which hung limply between his knees. He put it in his mouth and sucked in deeply.

"Where've you been the day, luv?"

I told him that I had walked into town and had a cup of tea with Peggy Ryan.

Pressing his lips together he blew smoke out of the corner of his mouth. "What did ya do ta yer head?" he asked, flicking the cigarette onto the ground in front of me.

I crushed it under my foot. "It's nothin', I just scraped it on a wall when I was runnin'."

He turned my face to look for himself, and when he was satisfied that it wasn't serious, he stood up. "I've got somethin' for ya in the caravan."

"Y'have? What is it?"

He pointed to the caravan. "See that parcel on yer bed? It's for you."

I ran to the bed and tore into the paper bag. It held a brown corduroy skirt. I held it up and looked at it.

"Oh, Daddy, it's lovely!"

He smiled, "There's more in the bag."

I put my hand in and pulled out a buttercup-yellow woollen sweater, a cable-twist pattern down each sleeve. I hugged it and put it down on the bed beside the skirt. There was still more in the bag: two pairs of soft, white cotton knickers, two matching undervests and two pairs of socks, one yellow and one pink. I ran to my father and hugged him.

"Oh, thank you, Daddy, thank you! Can I put them on now?"

"Certainly, Cushla, darlin'. It makes me happy seein' ye so pleased."

I couldn't express how happy I felt getting new clothes and especially the soft cotton knickers. While my father waited outside, I tried my new clothes on.

I removed my old clothes and stood naked while huge goosebumps that made me look like a plucked chicken covered my shivering body. First, I put on the soft knickers and a matching undervest. I ran my hands over my chest and bottom feeling the smoothness of the cotton. It felt silky-soft against my skin, so different from the prickly, irritating woollen ones that now lay on the floor. One at a time, I pulled on the yellow socks. They came right up to my knees. I put on the skirt and brushed the nap up and down with my hand. The beautiful sweater came last. I hugged myself with joy. I jumped out of the caravan and stood before my father, who smiled and sucked in his breath. "Ooh! Cushla, darlin', you look lovely!"

He gave me a hug and then held me at arm's length and said, "I should've done this long ago, but m'mind's ben too busy thinkin' about m'self and m'boxin'. I feel guilty, luv, about leavin' ya on yer own so much, but I think y'know that I love ya, and that I hav'ta train every day or I'd git outta shape in no time attal, and I'd be no good fer boxin' or nothin'."

I wrapped my arms around his waist and said as sweetly as I knew how, "I know that y'love me, Daddy, and I love you, too, so much so, that I hav'ta ask ya somethin'. Please don't fight t'morrow night. Y'got all busted up last time, and it pains m'heart ta see ya like that. Please stay home with me and we'll sit around the campfire together and sing songs."

He sighed, patted my hand and and stepped away. "That sounds lovely, Cushla, darlin', but ya must understand, I hav'ta go. Everybody's expectin' me t'go so they can win more money. They've got their money on that ugly big brute that beat me a fortnight ago, and they think the same things goin' ta happen t'morra. They've got the smell of my blood up their nose like a pack o' hungry wolves. But, he'll not beat me this time, fer I'm ready for 'im, and I'll be back here with two hundred pounds in my money belt, and d'ya know what that means, Cushla, darlin'?"

I knew, but I wouldn't say. Instead, I just looked at the pink scars on his knuckles.

"Well, nye, that means we will be goin' home to yer ma and David and wee William, and we could be on our way in a couple a days. So what d'ya think a that?"

"That's what I want more than anything, but . . ."

"No more buts. That's how it's goin' ta be, and we'll be home for Christmas to eat our plum duff and yella man."

The discussion was over.

"Nye, it must be time for supper, luv, so I'll go to Nora's and see what kinda grub we'll be gittin' the night."

My mind was a jumble of emotions. I gave in and sat on my bed running my hand down the velvety corduroy of my new skirt. I loved the feel and smell of my new clothes. It gave me a warm feeling that made me smile, imagining my father in a shop buying them for me. Much as I hated the thought of the fight, the thought of going home to my mother in a few days was a powerful consolation.

Suddenly, a wrecking-ball image came crashing through my happy thoughts, making me feel worried and unsettled. Embedded in my memory forever was the picture of my father, falling bleeding and lifeless to the concrete floor. I shook my head trying to dislodge this disturbing vision. It finally dissipated when I heard my father's humming getting louder as he entered the caravan with two steaming bowls. He placed them on the crate, rubbed his hands together in anticipation, and handed me a spoon.

"Dig in. It's rabbit stew. I think Billy's ben on a killin' spree this last couple o' days. I'm sure the rabbit population has taken a nosedive."

I really didn't like the thought of eating a poor wee rabbit, especially one murdered by Wild Billy, but I was starving, so I buried my conscience and ate every bit and licked the bowl afterwards.

There was no conversation while we ate, but when my father had finished, he placed his bowl back on the crate and said, "Nora's not well the day, she's in 'er bed. It was Annie that made the stew."

"What's the matter with 'er, is she bad?"

"Well, Harry Thornton, who was some kinda medic when he was in the army, says that he thinks she's got bronchitis and that she should have a mustard plaster on her chest the night. God, help 'er, cause I remember m'ma puttin' one on my chest and it burned like hell, and when she took the plaster off the next day, m'skin nearly came off with it. I moaned all night long. She thought it was with the pain in m'chest, but it was 'er bloody mustard plaster roastin' me. Anyway, I'm still alive, and I'm sure Nora'll be all right in a couple o' days."

"D'ya think I could go and see 'er and show 'er m'new clothes?"

"Aye, just don't stay too long and keep 'er from 'er sleep, 'cause she was given a powder when I went over ta git our supper."

I bounded over the crate and ran for the farmhouse. I had to pass Doreen and Jeannie, who were throwing a ball to each other in front of Doreen's caravan. I didn't turn to look at them. No use asking for trouble, but minding one's own business doesn't always guarantee that trouble won't invite itself to come along. If they couldn't inflict physical pain on you, their tongues could be just as lethal.

"Hey, ya wee shite, what's that yer wearin'? Looks like y'got some new clothes. Well, no matter, yer still ugly. Ya kin sprinkle rose petals on shite, but underneath it's still shite."

They both laughed, and then Doreen shouted, "Look at them skinny legs. I've seen better danglin' out of a nest!" They laughed even louder, and when I glanced over, they stuck their tongues out at me.

I sighed, relieved that at least this was only verbal abuse. Besides, I'd be leaving soon and I wouldn't miss those two wee torturers one bit.

I made myself walk at a leisurely pace, not wanting them to know I was afraid, more for my new clothes than for myself. I hoped that I would make it to the farmhouse without something being hurled at me. I heaved a great sigh of relief when I passed unscathed through the vines and into Nora's warm kitchen.

Archie Mallon was sitting at the table drinking black, strong-smelling tea out of a familiar chipped bowl. Stevie was sitting in front of the fire trying to pick something out of his finger. The fire was hissing and smoking as if someone had thrown something damp on it, and Nora's small form lay motionless on the mattress in the corner beside it.

"Hello, Archie, I've come to see how Nora's doin'."

He was holding his steaming bowl of tea with two hands, and after he slurped it, he put it back on the table. "She might be sleepin', but y'kin go over and see for yerself if y'want."

Before I reached her, Stevie turned and looked at me mournfully. "I've got a skelf in m'finger from carryin' that friggin' wood. It's in so friggin' deep I can't git it out and I've got no nails. Have you?"

"I do, but they're not very long."

"Well then, will y'have a go at tryin' ta git this friggin' thing out for me?"

Nora coughed a phlegmy cough. I really didn't want to be bothered with Stevie whose favourite word was obviously "friggin'," but I said I'd try.

I squeezed his finger, and he pulled it away. "Jezez, I didn't ask y'ta break m'friggin' finger."

Annoyed at his outburst, I gritted my teeth. "Y'hafta squeeze it ta get a wee end t' pull. D'ya want t'get it out or not?"

He narrowed his eyes at me. "All right then, have another go, but don't squeeze so friggin' hard."

I didn't have to squeeze it so hard this time because the end of the skelf was sticking out and with one pull it was out.

Stevie was suddenly happy. "Y'got it! It's out! Yer a quare wicked wee girl, Kathleen McKenna!" Then he jumped up sucking his finger and dashed out through the vines.

The sound of a coughing spasm from Nora in the corner told me that she wasn't asleep. I knelt by the mattress and whispered, "Nora, it's Kathleen. Is there anything I can get for you?"

Clearing her throat, she wheezed and answered quietly, "No thanks, luv. I only just threw the last dregs of a cup a tea on t'the fire.

I sat down on the mattress beside her and stroked her hot cheek with the back of my hand.

She looked and sounded exhausted. "Don't worry, luv, I'll be better in a couple o' days. It's m'chest. Every year at this time it gets bad—the damp weather, ya know."

She looked drowsy so I told her that I would leave her to sleep and that I would come to see her in the morning.

She closed her eyes and whispered, "Goodnight, luv. Annie'll be over in the mornin', and she'll see ta yer breakfast."

People in town were afraid of Nora; they thought she was evil. I knew differently. There she was, hardly able to breathe, and she was worried about my breakfast.

I didn't want to pass Doreen and Jeannie and face another volley of insults, so I walked behind the caravans until I reached my own. It was getting dark and I was afraid to meet Wild Billy, so I ran as fast as I could, almost afraid to breathe. Before going in for the night, I went into the woods a few feet behind the caravan, squatted down and peed behind my usual tree. Sitting in the dark peering through the steam rising from between my legs I thought to myself, "In the spring, I wouldn't be surprised if the leaves on this tree were yellow."

The caravan was dark, so I felt around the crate for matches and lit the candle. Smokey was sleeping on my bed and beside him was my slate with a note on it from my father. It said that he had gone to town and he'd see me in the morning. I sighed at the thought of spending another evening on my own. I took off my new clothes, folded them and put them on top of my raincoat in the corner. Crawling into bed and cuddling up with Smokey, I thought for the twentieth time how nice it was not to worry about rats falling on me in my sleep. When Smokey moved in, the rats moved out.

The next morning, Smokey woke me in his usual way, by bumping his head against my chin. I opened my eyes, and he meowed loudly and continued bumping. Sleepily, I pulled the blanket up over my head, but he was determined to get me up, so he climbed in under the blankets and started biting my chin. I gave in finally, and spoke to him with a sigh. "All right, Smokey, I'm gittin' up."

My father was already up and training with Tom. I remembered my new clothes and reached over behind my bed and dragged them in under the covers so that the damp, cold feeling would leave them before I put them on. But I was anxious to see how Nora was, so I dressed quickly and left the caravan. It was a cold, misty morning, and since nobody had a job to go to, the gypsies would stay in bed longer to keep warm. I heard Annie's coarse loud voice long before I reached the farmhouse.

"Hello, Annie, how's Nora this mornin'?"

"Ach, luv, she's still sleepin'. She had a terrible night with that oul cough. Sit you down there beside Stevie." She waddled over to the bubbling pot hanging in the fire and dipped the ladle in. Then she plopped a sizable dollop of thick porridge into a bowl, waddled back and put it in front of me and then did the same for Stevie.

"Git that inta yez, there's nothin like porridge ta stick ta yer ribs on a cold mornin' like this."

It was viscous and lumpy, and when Stevie put it into his mouth he stuck out his tongue and gagged. I didn't like it either, but I ate it, and it lay in my belly like a lump of lead the rest of the morning. Selfishly, I hoped Nora wouldn't be sick too long.

TWENTY-TWO

All day Friday I worried about my father's fight with Darcy Ferguson. Over and over the picture of his unconscious body collapsing onto the cement floor came into my mind. I could see the puddle of blood slowly spreading out from under his cheek.

My stomach lurched. I shook my head to rid my mind of that horrible image.

At least there was one diversion. I would be meeting Quin in a little while, and that lifted my spirits.

The sun was just disappearing behind the trees when my father came into the caravan to get his coat and hat. He kissed me on the cheek and told me to go over and get my supper from Annie. He said he wasn't eating because it wasn't good to fight with a full stomach.

"Don't you be worryin', luv. I'm goin' t'win the night, and we'll be on our way back home as soon as we can get a bus." There was a wee touch of nervousness in his voice.

I threw my arms around his neck and I held him tight. "I love ya, Daddy. Come back safe."

"Goodnight, luv. I'll see ya in the mornin'." Once more he kissed me gently on the cheek, picked up his hat, and in the style of Humphrey Bogart, tilted it over his right eye. He left the caravan whistling, "I'll Take You Home Again Kathleen." I listened until his lilting trill faded along with his footsteps into the night.

Walking over to the farmhouse to get my supper, I noticed that the camp was very quiet for this time on a Friday night. Usually people were bustling about gathering wood and debris for the bonfire and preparing for a lively gathering, but it had just started to rain, and with Nora being, sick there would be no partying tonight.

I brought my bowl of vegetable broth back to the caravan and ate listening to the patter of raindrops hitting the wooden roof. But the soft sound of a rain shower soon turned into a roar as heavy rain pounded steadily against the thin walls of the caravan.

Suddenly, I remembered Quin. He must be out there waiting for me. I thought I heard someone calling my name, but dismissed it, thinking it was just the hissing of the rain. Then I heard it again, along with thumping on the side of the caravan. I put my empty bowl on the floor and ran to the blanket. I parted it and stuck my head out into the rain. There was Quin, standing close to the caravan and soaked to the skin.

Holding the blanket out protecting myself from the rain, I asked in a loud whisper, "Is that you, Quin? Y'better git in here outta that rain."

Pushing strands of soaking wet hair away from his forehead, he replied, "Aye, I certainly will. I thought you'd forgotten me."

He pushed something white through the blanket then anchored his two hands on the doorframe and hoisted himself up. Sniffling and wiping his nose on his sleeve, he said, "I'm soaked t'the skin. I've ben waitin' out there in the pourin' rain fer about ten minutes to give yer da time ta git away. I saw him and that gypsy fella headin' off down the road."

He stopped talking, looked around the stark, cold, candlelit caravan. "Jezez, Kate, is this where you've ben livin'? There's nothin' here, just two wee beds."

"Just niver you mind, Quinton O'Hara, man of means and Lord of the Manor. M'da and me've done all right here, and besides, if he wins this fight the night, we won't be here much longer. We'll be leavin' for Belfast as soon as we kin git a bus."

He looked directly at me as if I'd said something alarming. "We've only just met, Kate, and I was happy to've made a new friend. I was hopin' we'd be friends for a while before you had ta leave."

It wasn't so much what he said but the way he said it that warmed my heart. I went over to him and took both his hands in mine and looked up into his glistening wet face and said, "No matter where I am or where I go, I'll always think of you as my knight-in-shining armour, and I'll niver forget you."

He dropped my hands and put his arms around my shoulders and hugged me, and I hugged him back. We were enjoying the warmth and security of each other's arms when he gave a little cough. "I won't let you forgit me, 'cause I have an auntie who lives in Belfast, and when m'ma and m'da go t'visit, I'll go and visit you."

Still enjoying the closeness of him, I said, "I'll tell m'mummy all about ya, and we'll look forward t'seein' ya in Belfast. Our home's no palace, but we've got more than two wee beds in it, and we'll be able to make ya a cup a tea."

The spell broken, I changed the subject. "Now we'd better git goin' if we're goin' t'see the fight."

I reached behind my bed for my Burberry raincoat and put it on, and he picked up the white thing off the floor and put it on his head. It was a helmet with a lamp in the middle. He pushed a little button at the side and the light came on.

"Quin, what on earth's that?"

He proudly told me that his da was a coalminer before he was a winda washer, and he had worn this down in the dark pits. He still wore it sometimes when he had to wash windas late at night. Quin turned off the light. "It's pitch black out there, so we can use it to see our way down the road."

We headed for the road to town through the woods at the back of the caravan. We walked like two zombies with our arms outstretched in front of us, feeling for trees in the total darkness. We didn't want to draw attention to ourselves by turning on his lamp. As our feet left the grassy woods, the familiar crunching stones told us we had reached the road. It was still raining, and heavy clouds covered the moon and stars, making the night so black we couldn't see the road in front of us.

Then Quin turned the little lamp on his helmet on. The light exploded into a funnel-shape burst of light illuminating ten feet in front of us. It was strange. You could only see the rain in the beam of light, and everything else was black. The rain had eased off a bit, but in no time we were both soaked and shivering. Quin took my hand and we started to run. It was like one of those frustrating dreams running down a tunnel hoping to reach the light at the end, but with each step the light got further away.

The blackness felt like a suffocating hood, but running with the wind blowing through my hair and soft cold rain sprinkling my face was liberating. It was much less threatening this time than the last when I had walked alone and terror-stricken down the lonely dark road.

Finally, a street lamp flickered at the edge of town. Quin quickly turned off the headlamp. We were out of breath and puffing hard from running, so we didn't say a word to each other as we made our way to Collin's Bakery. We stepped in the shadows a couple of times to let men pass. Soaked to the skin, we finally arrived at the entry leading to the bin shed. We crept along the walls in the shadows between the buildings and around to the back. I looked up and saw that the bottom pane of the window was still missing. I grabbed Quin's rain-soaked arm and pulled him close so that I could talk to him without having to shout over the rain. I pointed up to the window.

"That's where we're goin' ta watch the fight."

Quin looked up and said, "How d'ya git up there?"

The night sky was very black, and in the darkness you couldn't see the dented flour bin, but it was still in the same position I had left it. Trying to reassure him, I replied, "Don't worry, just follow me."

I climbed onto the unsteady bin. An inch or so of icy water had pooled on top, soaking the hem of my coat and new corduroy skirt. My hands and legs were wet and freezing from the cold, and I shivered as I hoisted myself onto the corrugated tin roof. Quin followed. We couldn't both fit into the windowwell, but if we lay on our bellies with our heads close together, we could see everything that was going on.

Quin put his head close to my ear and said as loudly as he dared, "We've got the best seat in the house."

I smiled and looked up over his head to the roof. I hadn't noticed before, but it had a bit of an overhang, which protected the top half of our bodies from the rain that was still pouring quite steadily.

Over the pounding and crashing waves hitting the seawall and the heavy rain drumming on the tin roof, we could barely hear the men's voices and laughter as they placed their bets with the man called Dennis. He was still wearing the red scarf, making him easy to spot in the crowd.

I felt a sense of déjà vu as the scene from a fortnight ago unfolded. The men were placing their bets. The same unkempt little man came in with the rope and told everybody to leave the centre of the floor. He passed the rope from man to man, forming a ring, and placed a chair, a jug of water and a bucket at opposite sides.

Quin pointed. "There's m'da. He's the oul geezer standin' holdin' on t'the back of the chair laughin' his head off, havin' a good oul yarn with the fella next to him. I told y'he'd be here."

Quin was excited and eager, but now that the adventure of getting here was over, I felt anxious and frightened. A jackhammer started up in my chest. I took a deep breath and swallowed hard. My father and Tom Sullivan had just walked into the centre of the ring followed by Darcy Ferguson himself, who looked even meaner and uglier than I remembered. I felt scared. I must've shown my fear in some way, because Quin, sensing my anxiety, took hold of my hand.

"Yer da's goin' t'show them the night who's the best fighter," he said confidently. "He knows what he's up against, and he's goin' ta win the night. You'll see."

I wished I could share his confidence. Even if he did win, he'd be bruised and bloody and maybe badly hurt at the end of it.

My father, naked from the waist up with the same white towel slung over his shoulder, was bouncing and throwing punches at a phantom opponent. Tom ducked under the rope to the outside of the ring as Danny Keogan entered into the centre.

He put his two hands in the air and shouted, "Can I have your attention, please?"

Then, louder, he shouted, "GENTLEMEN, PLEASE, CAN I HAVE YOUR ATTENTION?" The noise level of the rowdy crowd dropped off gradually until all we could hear was the rain on the tin roof.

We could barely hear Mr. Keogan as he introduced himself and said, "As you all know, 'Gypsy Jim' McKenna and Darcy Ferguson, also known as 'The Ballymena Brawler,' are here tonight for a rematch. Everybody knows the rules, and if y'all have placed yer bets, I won't waste anymore time talkin'."

He looked in turn to each opponent and asked, "Are ye ready?" Each man nodded that he was.

Mr. Keogan shouted, "Let the fight begin!" and quickly left the ring. The noise level rose immediately to an indecipherable ballyhoo as the men hooted and cheered on their champion.

As soon as Mr. Keogan left the ring, my father aggressively strode into the centre of the ring, pulled his right arm back and landed a mighty, full-force blow, dead centre to Darcy's grinning face.

If this had been a comic strip there would have been a big black question mark above the heads of the silent, stunned crowd with a collective "WHAT?" written in a bubble. Darcy went down hard, hitting his head on the cement floor. With blood pouring from his nose, he sat up immediately and shook his head. Blood and viscous red slobber sprayed all over the floor and spattered the faces and clothing of the men holding the rope. The men cheered as Darcy staggered to his feet.

As soon as he was upright, my father immediately charged and repeated the same punishing assault. Darcy fell hard for the second time. My father danced around the ring full of energy. At the end of the first round he was still untouched, except for the knuckles on his right hand.

Quin and I could hardly contain ourselves, and when Darcy went down, we banged our feet on the corrugated tin roof. Fortunately, the shouting, agitated men drowned us out. We giggled to ourselves, and I looked up into the heavens and smiled in relief, "Thank you, God, thank you."

Mr. Keogan came into the ring and said, "Seconds, come to yer man."

Tom Sullivan waited inside the rope with a white towel. My father sat down on the chair, and Tom poured water over his head and handed him some water in a tin cup, which he swished around his mouth and spat into the bucket. Tom dried his hair vigorously, and taking my father's right hand, dabbed the knuckles gently. I could see that they were bleeding, but there was no sign of pain on my father's face. In fact, he looked mighty pleased with himself.

Mr. Keogan looked at the two opponents and asked, "Are ye ready?"

Each man nodded yes. Darcy was warier this time as he circled the ring in a defensive posture.

My father strode up to Darcy and threw a strong hard punch at his face. Darcy ducked and my father missed him and was thrown off balance momentarily. Darcy seized the opportunity and lunged. He grabbed him by the hair and held his head while he punched him brutally in the face. Blood poured profusely from his nose and he went down on one knee. Splashes of red etched his chest and thigh as Darcy, his fist clenched tightly around a hank of my father's hair, kept punching him ruthlessly on the side of his head close to his right ear. The crowd was jubilant; loud cheers and whistles rose to fever pitch.

One loudmouth shouted thickly, "Take the fuckin' gypsy down, Darcy! Beat the b'jesus out of 'im like y'did last time!"

I put my hands over my eyes. I whispered to Quin, "I can't look."

Quin tried to reassure me. "In a minute you'll see he'll be back on 'is feet, teachin' that oul divil a lesson he'll not soon forget."

The crowd was shouting and whistling, and I heard the same voice shout, "Hey, Darcy, just rip his fuckin' head off."

I opened my eyes slowly. My father was struggling to get to his feet and trying to free his hair from Darcy's grip. His face contorted in pain, he drove his fist into the pit of Darcy's stomach, just above the groin. Darcy seemed oblivious and twisted and pulled even harder. The next blow was aimed lower and caught Darcy in a most vulnerable spot. Darcy's fingers sprang open, and my father was free. Darcy doubled over, clutching his groin with both hands and fell to his knees.

The crowd's mood changed predictably.

Instantly, my father charged Darcy, pulverizing his cheek with a solid right hook. Immediately, he followed with a tooth-rattling left uppercut to his chin, and finally, with one mighty, bone-crunching solid right punch, dead centre to Darcy's lacerated nose, the big man went down. And stayed down. My father had knocked him out.

Mr. Keogan ducked under the ropes and went over to the unconscious man lying on the cold, blood-spattered concrete floor. He knelt down and put his ear close to Darcy's nose, checking to see if he was still breathing. My father was shaking his head and holding his right ear. Although he was glad to win, he didn't know at the time that he would have to live with a constant reminder of this brutal contest. He would be deaf in his right ear for the rest of his life. Tom came and stood beside him and threw the towel around his shoulders.

Mr. Keogan stood up, counted to ten, and lifted my father's hand in the air and declared him the winner.

Loud boos from the crowd indicated that the crowd was definitely not pleased with the outcome. Other than a big blue bruise on his right cheek, my father's face wasn't too badly damaged at all. He was the one that had done most of the punching this time.

Quin said, with a note of urgency in his voice which broke my concentration, "Come on, Kate, we've got to get to the caravan before yer da, so we'd better git outta here now."

My heart was thumping hard against my chest. I wanted to run down there and throw my arms about him and tell my father how proud I felt. I knew I couldn't do that so I turned to Quin and said, choking back tears, "Oh, Quin, I love m'daddy and I want to be with 'im so much m'heart aches."

Quin's impatient voice was the voice of reason. He grabbed my wet, cold hand. "Well, Kate, if we don't leave right this minute, you'll have more than an achin' heart to contend with, so come on, let's go."

He put the white helmet on his head, gave it a thump on top to secure it well, and pulled me to my feet. We slid off the roof one at a time onto the flour bin, jumped to the wet, muddy ground, and ran in the shadows of the houses until we were on the road to the camp.

I hardly noticed how dark it was being with Quin. Holding his hand as we ran gave me a sense of security and protection. I remembered how frightening the least little sound was when I was on my own.

When we passed the last lamp at the edge of town, Quin turned on the headlamp. I laughed. He really did look ridiculous in the pitch black. All I could see was a bobbing beam of white light with rain lashing through it. I suppressed my laughter and thought to myself how very glad I was that Quin had seen the fight and he was with me now.

We were out of breath from running up the hill, soaked to the skin and shivering, but I hardly felt the cold as I remembered Mr. Keogan holding up my father's arm and proclaiming him the winner.

In a few days I would be going home to my mother, and despite the rain, just thinking of her soft voice and loving smile warmed me all over.

We were out of breath running and gasping, so we didn't say a word to each other. When we got to the top of the hill, Quin switched off the lamp, and we looked back for headlights and listened for the sound of a car engine labouring up the hill. There wasn't a sound, so we relaxed our vigil and slowly walked through the trees to the caravan.

I climbed the rickety step and held the blanket open for Quin. I told him he could come in for a few minutes. He leaped in through the door. Once inside I started to shake. I felt my way between the beds to light the candle. Suddenly, a fiendish howl filled the caravan.

"Jezez! What the bloody hell was that?" Quin shouted.

I was shaking harder than ever and my heart was pounding. I had stood on Smokey's tail, not knowing that he had been sleeping on my dress under the bed with his tail sticking out. His piercing shriek shattered the silent darkness, scaring the life out of both of us.

"I've stood on my poor wee cat's tail."

I reached forward and felt for the candle and matches. I struck the match, but my hand was shaking so violently I couldn't light the candle.

Quin came over and took the match from me and lit the stubby candle. In an instant the caravan was bathed in soft yellow light.

We both burst into relieved laughter.

He shook his head and said, "Jezez, Kate, I thought I was sent for then."

I was still shivering so hard, I was having trouble with the buttons of my wet coat. Quin moved my hands away and undid the buttons. He helped me take it off and threw it in the corner. Then he pulled the blanket off my bed and wrapped me in it and put his arms around me and rubbed my back vigorously. I opened the blanket and put it around him and drew him inside. We clung to each other wrapped in the warmth of the blanket for a couple of minutes, and then I looked up at him and saw that he still had his white helmet on.

I laughed and so did Quin. We lost our balance and fell onto the bed.

Still laughing, he shook his head, "What an ejit. There you were feelin' yer way in the pitch black to light the candle when all I had to do was turn on the bleedin' lamp!"

I was enjoying the laughter and the closeness of him lying on my bed when suddenly he sat bolt upright, holding his hand up to silence me. "Shush! I think I hear somethin'!" We held our breath and looked at each other and in unison droned, "A car!"

Untangling himself from the blanket, Quin said, "I'd better git goin'."

At the door of the caravan Quin said, "That was a quare good night we had, yer da winnin' an all."

I took his hand and looked directly into his eyes and smiled gratefully. "Aye, it was indeed, and I want ta thank ya for comin' with me." Still holding his hand, I leaned over and kissed him lightly on the lips.

Embarrassed, he shifted his eyes downward and drew his fingertips across his lips.

"Ach, don't mention it, I had a good time m'self."

Then he jumped over the crate and turned and looked up at me. Pushing his helmet to the back of his head, he hesitated a moment as if there was something else he wanted to say. But the roar of a car engine and the flash of headlights through the trees interrupted his thoughts and hastily he said, "Good night, Kate," and disappeared into the night just before the car reached the circle of caravans.

Only seconds after he had been swallowed up by the darkness, I heard voices getting closer and closer. The rain had stopped, and I was glad. Quin wouldn't get any wetter going home alone in the dark. Quickly I shed my new corduroy skirt and spread it out on the floor at the foot of my bed. I jumped in and covered myself with the damp blanket.

Just outside the door of the caravan, my father said, "Thanks, Tom, I was glad ta have ya in m'corner."

I heard the rattling of paper and then Tom's incredulous voice said, "But, Jimmy, fifty quid!"

My father's voice registered his pleasure at Tom's surprise. "Nye you an Ginny kin git married and live happily ever after, so ta speak."

Tom was apparently struck dumb by my father's generosity, but finally he spoke, "Thanks very much, Jimmy, but I'd a done it fer nothin'. You've ben a good friend, and I hate ta see ya leavin'. As fer gittin' married, I'll havta think about that, but this could be m'ticket outta here, ya niver know. Maybe I'll take m'self off to Australia and git a job on a sheep farm or somethin'."

Still straining my ears to hear what was being said, I heard my father say, "Well, Tom, I'm plannin' t'leave Ireland and take m'family somewhere away from here. Maybe Canada. So once I'm established, I'll gladly help y'out any way I can, if y'have a mind t'come. It would probably do y'good t'git away from this life and start fresh in a new country."

My mind was too full of thoughts to hear what Tom's reply was. Leaving Ireland still bothered me, but the thought of seeing my mother and brothers pushed the threat of Canada right out of my mind. I allowed myself to think what it would be like to sleep in my own bed. I pictured all of us sitting around the table eating dinner together, my mother and father talking and making plans, and my two brothers and I giggling over something silly. It seemed like I had been waiting forever for this time to come. I could hardly keep from leaping out of bed and going to my father.

Although I was happy to be leaving the gypsies, I would definitely miss some aspects of my life here. I would miss Nora, who had been a substitute granny and good friend. Then there was Peggy Ryan, whom I might never get to see again. But I felt saddest when I thought about Quin. His friendship was special, the sharer of the very best adventure of my gypsy life. I didn't like to think that I might never see him again, either. He was my knight-in-shining-armour, and I couldn't bear to think of life without him now.

I was so deep in thought that I didn't hear my father come in. Suddenly he was just there, shuffling around in the dark, the smell of his smokey clothing filling the caravan. When he was settled in bed, I spoke into the darkness.

"Daddy?"

"What, luv?"

"Did y'win?"

Even in the dark, pride coloured what he said. "Aye, luv, I did. I won eighty quid the night so that means I've got over two hundred quid in m'money belt and y'know what that means, nye don't ye? I'll be goin' in ta Ballymacruise on Monday mornin' ta see when we kin git a bus to Belfast. What d'ya think a that nye, Cushla, darlin'?"

"Oh, Daddy, it'll be a dream come true! I kin hardly wait till Monday."

I couldn't get warm. My blanket was damp from having been wrapped around two sopping teenagers. Teeth chattering from the cold as well as from excitement, I asked, "Daddy, kin I git in with ya for a minute till I warm up? Yer not too sore, are ya?"

"No, Cushla, darlin', I'm not too sore. Come on over an git warmed."

I crawled under the blanket, which he held up for me. I felt warm and safe, and I slept contented until the first rays of light shone through the cracks in the caravan. I lay still, not wanting to disturb him, and getting out from under the warm blanket didn't seem like a good idea at the time either.

When my father woke up, he put his hand to his right ear. He shook his head and groaned. "That oul divil Ferguson's nearly deafened me. Kept punchin' me in the ear, so 'e did, nye all I kin hear is ringin' and buzzin'."

I put my hand on his ear.

"Ach, it'll go away in a day or two," he said, trying to ease my concern. But it never went away. Years later he found out that the punishing blows to the side of his head had ruptured his eardrum.

I coaxed myself out from under the warm blanket and hugged myself as I shivered. I reached below the bed for my everyday dress. Smokey had been sleeping on it and the hem of the skirt was covered in grey hairs. I brushed them off the best I could, put it on and surreptitiously tucked the wet bundle of new clothes under my arm. My father didn't notice. He was lighting a cigarette. Smoke plumed upwards from his puckered lips, and as I passed he said, "Tell Nora or Annie that I'll be over in a wee while, all right, luv?"

I pulled open the blanket to leave, and a shaft of light fell on my father's bed. The knuckles of his right hand were puffy and raw and crusted with blood, and there was an angry red and purple bruise on his right cheekbone. I got a strange feeling in the pit of my stomach remembering Darcy pummelling the side of his face, over and over. I looked at his ear as though there was something wrong with it and said in a normal tone, "Sure, I'll tell 'er."

TWENTY-THREE

Squatting down behind my favourite tree to pee, I counted how many times I would use this spot before we left for home. Probably no more than seven. In Belfast, this now-familiar routine would seem primitive and quaint. I wiped myself on the hem of my skirt and headed to the farmhouse.

I was very happy to see Nora sitting in the chair beside the fire. Annie was bent over the big black cauldron, her plump behind jiggling as she stirred the thick porridge with enthusiasm. Archie was sleeping in the corner with a brown crockery jug cradled in his left arm. I spread my wet clothes on a chair beside the fire.

"Come an sit yerself down, luv. The porridge's nearly ready," Annie shouted.

The thought of eating Annie's thick, salty porridge didn't exactly whet my appetite, but after my adventure and with all my good news, I was ready to eat anything.

"Are y'better, Nora?" I laid my hand on her bony shoulder.

She looked at me with dark, watery eyes and smiled, "M'fever's broken, luv, so I'll be on m'feet in no time attal."

"I was worried about ye."

Adjusting her shawl around her shoulders, she said, "Ach, it'd take more than a wee cough to put me in the ground."

Annie looked around and agreed. "Aye, it would indeed. You've ben through a hell of a lot worse than that in yur day."

Nora glanced at me suspiciously. "Why's yer clothes all wet? Did y'happen t'take a wee walk inta town last night?

I went over to the table and took a seat close to the door. "Yes, Nora, I did and I'm glad, 'cause m'da won."

"He did!" Her dark eyes widened as she leaned forward in her chair.

"Y'mean 'e beat that big brute Ferguson? I know that yer da's a quare good fighter, but I had m'doubts about him winnin', 'cause, from what I hear, that Ferguson's a quare nasty fella and would do anything t'win."

So she hadn't known the future, then.

Annie waddled over with a steaming bowl of thick porridge. She put it down in front of me and handed me a spoon. "Git that in t'ya nye, luv."

Trying to look enthusiastic I mumbled, "Thanks, Annie."

I ate the salty globs of porridge as fast as I could and stood beside the fire to get warm. Then I went outside feeling lighthearted and happy with thoughts of going home. But I didn't go back to the caravan. If I was leaving Monday, I wanted to see Quin one more time. For the second time in twelve hours, I headed into town.

The morning was misty but promised fair weather, and as I walked down the stony road, I took stock of my gypsy life: that awful time when I had to go to school and had been beaten by Mr. Spencer for being a gypsy; going to court and appearing before a judge and standing up for my father; Peggy Ryan sneaking off to tell me about the death of Mr. Spencer and wondering if Nora and her gypsy magic had anything to do with it; the scary solitary excursion to watch the first fight, and the very different excursion with Quin to watch my father beat Darcy Ferguson. So much had happened. I had become a different person since leaving the security of my home. In Belfast I rarely went anywhere without my mother. I never ventured far from home.

I was lost in my thoughts, which had come full circle when I heard someone calling, "Kate!" Someone who could only be Quin was waving through the mist and shouting. Nobody but Quin called me Kate. I ran down the hill gathering up so much speed that Quin had to grab my arm to slow me down.

We laughed as we spun around from the momentum, and then he took my hand and we walked to the ruins of the old stone church. We went up the path and found the same big square stone that we had sat on the first day we met. With sadness changing the tone of his usual lilting happy-go-lucky voice, he said, "Well, Kate, we're back where we started. You'll be leavin' in a couple a days, and I'll be back to havin' nothin' to look forward to." His Adam's apple bobbed as he swallowed hard, and his voice wavered as he said, "Your m'best friend, Kate, and I just want ya t'know that I'll niver forget ya."

Tears welled up in my eyes and spilled over onto my cheeks.

"I won't forget you either, Quin."

Our combined misery threatened to carry us away into melodrama, so I brushed my tears away with my fingertips and wiped my nose on the end of my sleeve. I tried to lighten up the mood a bit by saying, "But we have today, and we can spend the whole day together if you like."

"I can't, Kate, I've got to go with m'da to help 'im wash windas. I go with 'im every Saturday and Sunday as well, so this'll be the last time I'll see ya."

I couldn't accept this being the last I'd see of Quin. "No, Quin," I said, trying to convince both of us. "It won't be the last time. You said that sometimes y'come ta Belfast t'see yer aunt. Well y'kin come an visit me then. You're my best friend, too, and I don't want this ta be the last time that we'll see each other."

He pulled me towards him and we hugged each other, not saying anything for a few minutes, and then Quin stood up.

"I've got t'go, Kate. M'da's waitin' fer me."

Looking down at me, and trying to keep his emotions under control, he said. "Do y'want me to walk ya to the road?"

I didn't trust myself not to cry, so I said, "No, I want to sit here for a wee minute or two."

He reached down and took hold of my two hands and pulled me to my feet. We stood looking at each other, not knowing what to say and not wanting our time together to end. I dropped his hands and reached around my neck and took my shell necklace off. I placed it around his neck and said, "This'll help y'to remember me."

Taking hold of my hands once again and with tears glistening in his eyes, he kissed me gently on the cheek and said softly, "I'll not be needin' anything to help me remember you, 'cause you'll always be in m'heart." He dropped my hands and with sadness changing the tone of his voice said, "Goodbye, Kate." And then he ran up the road. Before he disappeared around the trees I shouted, "Remember I live on Nore Street!"

I sat in the ruins, my eyes brimming over with tears. The trees were shrouded in early morning mist, making the scene before me look like one of those blurry French paintings. I couldn't stay there much longer. I was starting to shiver, and the empty feeling of loss made my heart ache. I comforted myself thinking that Quin would certainly come to visit, not only me, but my whole family.

I took a deep breath, closed my eyes and thought of my mother. The sadness of the last few moments lifted as I thought of how she would enfold me in her arms. I could almost feel the softness of her cheek, wet with tears of joy against mine.

In just a couple of days we would be together, and I promised myself that nothing in this world would take me away from her again.

As I left the old church ruins, I thought to myself, this would always be a special place for me, because it was here that I first met Quin.

I set out for Peggy's house.

From the top of the hill I saw Peggy and her mother closing their garden gate behind them, so I ran down the hill waving and shouting.

"Peggy, wait!"

Both Peggy and her mother turned around, and even from a distance I could tell that they both had broad smiles on their faces when they saw me.

"Ach, Kathleen, I wish I'd known you were comin'. M'mummy and me are goin' inta town ta do a wee bit a Christmas shappin."

"It's all right," I said to Peggy, "I'll not be stayin'. I've just come t'say goodbye. M'daddy an me are goin' home on Monday!"

"Oh, Kathleen, y'must be so happy," Peggy said. She hugged me for a minute and then kept holding my hand.

"I didn't want t'go without sayin' goodbye. You've been a good friend to me, and I wanted ta tell ya that I'd niver forgit ya."

"Aye, well, I'll not forget you either, but I know how much y'miss yer mother, so I'm very glad yer goin' home an' all."

Mrs. Ryan said, "Cheerio, luv, and God bless ye."

Peggy let go of my hand to take her mother's, and they walked away. At the bottom of the street they turned around and waved.

With no one left to visit, I walked back to the gypsy camp in time to see Smokey jogging along with a mouse dangling from his mouth. He was such a good hunter. I never had to worry about feeding him. I wondered how he was going to like being a city cat.

I was just about to go into the caravan when Doreen and Jeannie approached me. They looked as unkempt and sounded as unfriendly as ever. Doreen said, "So I hear yer leavin'."

I matched my tone of voice to hers. "Aye, in a couple a days."

"Well," she said tartly, "good riddance. Niver would be too soon if I had to look at yer ugly face again."

Jeannie chimed in, "Aye, an I'll be glad t'see y'go as well."

"Not half as glad as I will be ta see the last o' you two."

And thus we three said our goodbyes.

TWENTY-FOUR

Saturday night the gypsies had their usual *ceilidh* with dancing and singing around a bonfire. Archie Mallon made an official anouncement about our departure, though word had already reached everyone in the camp. Everybody drank to our health and wished us a safe journey back home. I stayed for a little while, but when rain and sleet started, I went back to the caravan to bed. I listened to the singing and laughter, eventually falling asleep with Smokey. As usual after a party, my father came stumbling in drunk and singing, "That's Why I Love Mary, the Rose of Tralee."

When I went out to pee the next morning, the ground was covered with snow. My father was recuperating from his overindulgence the night before, and I was thinking about going home.

Monday, I woke up to the wind screaming around the corners of the caravan. I looked through a crack to see a flurry of sleet and hail. I went to see Nora. She was back to her old self and smiled her toothless smile when I brushed aside the vines.

"Mornin', luv,"

"You're better! Oh, Nora, it's grand t'see ya lookin' so well!"

"Ach aye, luv, I'm better, to be sure. Nye you sit yerself down and have yer bread and milk. It'll probably be the last time."

I sat down at the table deep in thought. Bittersweet emotions plagued me when I thought of leaving the gypsies. I was happy and sad at the same time. I could hardly wait to see my mother again, but I would miss Nora. Her strength, her mystery and her magic had enveloped me and sustained me through a difficult and puzzling time of my life. Without her I would have been lost.

Intuitively, as though she read my thoughts, she said, "Nye, luv, don't dwell on the past. Ye can't change it, but the future's whativer y'make of it. Go on t'yer next adventure and make the most of whatever life offers, and if ya fail at somethin', don't give up—that just means that that somethin' needs t'be improved. M'cards tell me that you'll have a good, long and happy life. Don't be sad leavin' me, cause m'memory'll be with y'always, and your memory'll be with me foriver. Nye eat yer breakfast 'fore it gits cold."

Tears were just a heartbeat away. But I ate the hot, sweet mixture with a great deal of pleasure when I remembered Annie's porridge. When I had finished, I went over to Nora and put my arms around her.

"Thank you, Nora, for everything. Maybe one day I'll come back and visit ye."

She gently pushed me away, and holding on to my shoulders and looking directly into my eyes, she said, "No, y'won't, fer you'll not be in Ireland that long. Life's got big plans fer ya, and they don't include travellin' with a band o' gypsies. So go on with ya now."

For such a thin, bony old woman, Nora hugged me as warmly and comfortingly as a mother. I put my arms around her thin waist and hugged her close for the last time. I had a lump in my throat that felt like a lump of coal. "Oh, Nora, I'll miss y'more than words can say." My throat was burning from holding back tears, so I kissed her on the cheek and looked into her dark eyes that also had become glassy and tear-filled. I whispered a final goodbye. I quickly turned and went out through the vine-covered doorway for the last time.

TWENTY-FIVE

Back at the caravan, my father was shaving in the candlelight.

"Y'look like you've ben cryin', luv. Don't tell me yer sad at leavin' this place nye, are ye?"

"No, I'm not sad at leavin', but I just said goodbye to Nora, and I'm goin' t'miss 'er. She's ben like a granny t'me."

"Ach, aye," he said sympathetically, wiping his face with the bottom of his shirt. "Both herself and Archie have ben very decent to us, but just think, luv, you'll be seein' your ma and yer brothers t'night. Surely that makes y'happy. Will y'be comin' inta town with me to see about a bus?"

The reality of going home struck with a force that was staggering.

"Aye, that certainly makes me feel happier, and I do want to go inta town with ya!"

I put on my new clothes and my Burberry raincoat. I pulled my knee socks up as far as they would go, and then we headed off down the road. We marched as we did that first day when we left Belfast. Except this time I wasn't crying.

At the bus station, my father approached a stern-looking man with very black hair and thick bushy eyebrows, sitting behind a glass window with a round hole in the middle. Through the hole he asked when the next bus was leaving for Belfast.

The man smiled, softening the harshness of his face, and he answered politely, "You've just missed one, and the next one's not until a quarter past three this afternoon."

My father thanked him and looked at the clock behind the desk. "It's half past eleven, so we'll have time to go to the pub for a wee sandwich or somethin'. Do y'fancy that, Cushla, darlin'?"

I was adjusting fast to this new affluence and enthusiastically replied, "Oh, yes, that would be nice."

We went to Mulligan's pub and had fish and chips. They were just as good as they were the first time, but I enjoyed them even more than that other, long-ago time when I was in so much pain.

Everyone in the pub nodded or called out to my father, and when we finished he went from the table, saying goodbye and shaking hands with everybody. Men wanted to buy him drinks, but he thanked them and declined.

Instead of going right back to camp, my father said he wanted to visit a wee shop around the corner. A short walk later we arrived at small dimly lit store with wire mesh covering its windows. Three brass balls hung over the front door.

"Hi ya, Jimmy," the pawnbroker said. "I know what you'll be after since y'won that money."

He took a key from his pocket and opened a glass case behind the cash register. He lifted out a red leather, heart-shaped box and opened it. The inside was lined with shiny white satin, and nestled in the middle was a string of creamy white pearls.

"Aye, Sammy, that's the one." My father put a ten-pound note on the counter.

Sammy handed the box to my father. "Well, Jimmy, it's been nice knowin' ye. I wish you and your family all the best, and have a Happy Christmas." Looking down at me he added, "And you, too, lass."

My father tucked the box into the inside pocket of his coat and shook the man's hand.

"Thanks, Sammy, and the same to you and yours."

There was an inch or so of wet snow on the road as we headed back to the gypsy camp. Sleet and hail pelted our backs. My feet were wet and cold, but tonight I'd be sitting in front of the fire in my own house enjoying my family all together again.

It was one o'clock when we got back to the caravan for the last time. My father packed up his few belongings and went to say goodbye to Nora, Archie and Tom. Smokey and I lay on the bed and waited.

Not long after, my father poked his head through the doorway. "Well, Cushla, darlin', it's time to leave this place and go home."

Those words made me feel light and warm, like an angel had enveloped me in her wings and lifted me up, body and soul, to the sun. I was so happy, tears sprang to my eyes, and I rushed at him and hugged him, proclaiming that it was the happiest day of my life.

I picked up Smokey and put him into my coat. At the door of the caravan, I turned and had one last look at our gypsy home. Then I jumped over the crate and took my father's hand.

Nora, Archie, Tom, Annie and Ginny were standing outside the old farmhouse. They waved until we were out of sight. I know because I kept turning around for a last look until the road turned and I couldn't see them anymore.

It was ten minutes to three when we got to the bus depot. My father bought our tickets, and we sat on a hard, rickety bench until the conductor called for passengers going to Belfast. We lined up with the others and filed one-by-one into the bus.

I chose a window seat in the middle. Smokey was fast asleep and purring loudly. My father had bought a *Belfast Telegraph* and was wide-eyed with the pleasure of reading a current newspaper when the bus driver came in and closed the doors. He turned on the engine, and a hundred butterflies started fluttering around in the pit of my stomach. I thought I might die before the bus started moving and I breathed again. We were really going home.

I settled down ready for my journey and looked out the window. Movement up the street caught my eye and I blinked a couple of times to make sure I wasn't seeing things, but running up the street was Quin. He looked like he had been running for a long time. He was pumping his legs as fast as he could and breathing hard with one hand holding his side.

The bus was just pulling out of the station when he stopped, bent over and put his hands on his knees gasping for air. I turned around pressing my face to the window and waved. Recovering his breath, he started running after the bus. He was getting close enough for me to see the shell necklace bouncing around his neck. He ran until the bus picked up too much speed for him to keep up.

I crushed passed my father and ran to the back of the bus. An elderly couple sitting in the middle of the back seat moved aside sensing my urgency. Anxiously I climbed into the space between them and sat on my knees waving until he was too far away for me to see him any longer.

Seeing him left me unsettled. Did he just want to say goodbye again, or was there something important he wanted to say? I'll never know what it was that he wanted.

An overwhelming feeling of regret disturbed me as I slowly made my way back to my seat beside my father. He asked me what I had run to the back of the bus so quickly for. I just told him that I thought I had seen someone I knew. I had never told him about Quin and there was no point to his knowing now.

On the way back to Belfast and home, my father and I reminisced about our three and a half months with the gypsies. He had promised that we would be home for Christmas, and he had kept his promise. He started to talk about a new life in Canada or California, but I couldn't think that far ahead. I was going home to my mother, and soon I would see my brothers, and that was enough food for thought.

My life with the gypsies had sometimes been unbearable, but through hardship and absolute determination by my father not to return home empty-handed, we developed a loving, respectful relationship that lasted a lifetime, and I learned that there is no greater reward in life than true friendship.

Author's Note

As a child, I lived with my family in the first house on Nore Street in Belfast, Northern Ireland. The streets in this section of Belfast were named after rivers in Ireland. Each street had twenty-four identical brick houses, twelve on each side of the street. The only difference between them was that some had lacy white curtains, some had blinds with novelty pull strings and some had plain white sheer curtains crossed in the middle. Behind closed doors there was a family trying to survive on little or no money.

We were poor, but my parents did their best to provide a stable home. Our furniture was sparse and practical, but we had two very unusual pieces that stood out like roses in a cabbage patch. One was a beautiful mahogany piano, and the other was a large glass case in which colourful stuffed birds were displayed. These items, which belonged to my grandfather, James Bell, were sold to pay for our passage to Canada. My grandfather had been born into a wealthy family who owned and operated a funeral home. He was the eldest son, but did not want to pursue a career in the undertaking business, so his father disinherited him and forced him to leave. His family let him take the piano, which he played beautifully, the glass display case and a gold watch. He was artistic and loved working with wood, so he became a carpenter.

My mother, Molly Bell, her four brothers and two sisters were raised in this house, and when her mother and father passed away, she stayed in the family home. She married my father, who lived on the opposite side of Nore Street, and they lived in this house with my two brothers and me until we left for Canada.

My father was the youngest of nine children—eight boys and one girl. He joined the British Army when he was eighteen and married my mother at twenty-three. After he left the army he worked at Harland and Wolfe Shipyards in Belfast as a steamfitter and welder. He thought he would be there for life, like his father, but after seven years he was laid off. His father, David McKnight, had worked in the shipyard since he was fourteen, and as a young man, worked on the *Titanic* as a labourer.

Losing his job at the shipyard was devastating for my father. He had three young children to feed and care for: my brothers Jim and baby George and myself.

My brothers were handsome children with honey-blond hair. Jim's hair was shoulder-length and curly, and his eyes were a lovely grey-blue. George's hair was fine and wispy, but his thick dark eyelashes framed the brightest eyes, the colour of Irish moss in the sunshine.

I was small for my age, but I made up for my lack of size by my independent spirit. Precocious and outspoken, I could hold my own in any situation.

When my father was in India, still fighting with the British Army, my mother, two cousins and I were evacuated out of Belfast to a gypsy caravan on the outskirts of a town called Cookstown. My mother was looking after her brother Walter's children while he was in India also fighting with the British Army. Their mother had died at twenty-six of a brain aneurism. Nora and Archie are based on the two people in charge of the gypsy camp.

Belfast in the 1950s was still suffering from the ravages of World War II, and there wasn't enough of anything, except hunger and worry. Mothers worried about how they were going to feed and clothe their children. Fathers worried about getting a job so that they could take care of their families. Children worried about their mothers and fathers worrying.

I was four years old the first time I saw my father, a tall stranger in a soldier's uniform. I grew to love and trust that once frightening stranger, and after losing his job at Harland and Wolfe Shipyards, my father was forced to leave home in search of work. He left Belfast on a cold September morning. Walking from town to town, and from factory to factory, my father struggled against losing heart each time he was told he wasn't needed.

After two weeks on the road, his money was spent and his food was gone. Discouraged and exhausted from sleeping in meadows and under bridges, he reluctantly joined a band of gypsies for survival.

Cushla is based on true events.

About the Author

Elizabeth Radmore was born in Belfast, Northern Ireland, to James and Mollie McKnight. In 1951, her father emigrated alone to Canada, so that he could find a job and a home for his wife and three children: Elizabeth, Jim and George. The family settled and prospered in Ottawa, and although James and Mollie have since passed away, Elizabeth remains close to her brothers.

Elizabeth has previously published a collection of poetry, winning an Editor's Choice Award for one of the poems, and an article about the dangers lurking in our everyday environment that was distributed nationally. *Cushla* is her first novel.

Elizabeth and her husband live in Ottawa with their calico cat "Cali" and their beloved black Lab, Chelsea. Elizabeth's children, Jason, Natalie and Rachel, are grown, and live close by with families of their own.